W9-BGY-712

THE DEALINGS OF
DANIEL KESSERICH

THE DEALINGS OF DANIEL KESSERICH

A STUDY OF THE MASS-INSANITY AT SMITHVILLE

FRITZ LEIBER

Illustrations by Jason Van Hollander

A TOM DOHERTY ASSOCIATES BOOK

NEW YORK

This is a work of fiction. All the characters and events portrayed in this novel are either fictitious or are used fictitiously.

THE DEALINGS OF DANIEL KESSERICH

This book is printed on acid-free paper.

Edited by David G. Hartwell

A Tor Book
Published by Tom Doherty Associates, Inc.
175 Fifth Avenue
New York, NY 10010

Tor Books on the World Wide Web:

http://www.tor.com

Tor® is a registered trademark of Tom Doherty Associates, Inc.

Design by Ann Gold

Library of Congress Cataloging-in-Publication Data

Leiber, Fritz, 1910–1992

The dealings of Daniel Kesserich / Fritz Leiber.

p. cm.

"A Tom Doherty Associates book."

ISBN 0-312-85408-0

I. Title.

PS3523.E4583D39 1997

813'.54—dc20 96-44853

CIP

First Edition: March 1997

Printed in the United States of America

0 9 8 7 6 5 4 3 2 1

CONTENTS

CONTENTS

FOREWORD

Let me first explain that I have not intentionally written this as an explanation for the curious or as a warning to the overly curious. No. I merely wanted to make a permanent account of certain singular experiences that were beginning to be too much for my unaided memory. I wanted to have something to refer to, an anchor of fact to hold me down when my imagination began to wander too dangerously far afield. Being an author by profession I made this "anchor of fact" into, not a series of notes, but a story.

No one, you see, is curious about the mass-insanity at Smithville for no one knows even of its occurrence—that is, no one except the inhabitants of that ominous town and they are all too eager to forget. Some of them have already forgotten, forced themselves to forget. A stranger, to learn anything, would have to work through several back issues of the local newspaper and then obtain from the inhabitants old gossip and tales, tales that they are singularly unwilling to recount. Even then he would have only a hint.

But I was on the scene at the crucial time.

Nor, as I have said, would it be of any avail for me to warn the overly curious against prying too closely into that puzzling group of events that touched obscurely, but with shivering danger, upon the teetering, black foundations of our threatened universe.

No, when I wrote the body of this narrative, I wanted neither to warn nor to explain, or—strangest—to see it sold and printed. Not that I am adverse to money making. But, you see, at that time the story had no ending or, to be precise, it ended with a gigantic question mark. And stories are required to have reasonable endings.

At that time the last section was the one I have entitled "The Final Outburst."

Now there are two additional chapters. These two chapters give a hideously convincing explanation of what was before only disturbingly enigmatical. The claims made in them may be criticized and ridiculed by certain of the scientifically minded. Nevertheless, I myself find that I must accept them or accept nothing at all, save admission of defeat in the face of the inexplicable.

And I was on the scene.

For what happened at Smithville *is* inexplicable in terms of mankind's present knowledge. That is, inexplicable to everyone except possibly one man and he had more than mankind's present knowledge. Or, at least, I am led to believe so.

How those last two chapters came into my hands will be told in due course.

So I trust I have now explained why this story is being published. The two final chapters gave it an ending, made it salable—and I am one who is always willing to sell.

And so my little narrative goes out into the world, the little narrative that was written only to bring order into a black chaos of events in the real world and a threatening chaos of hypotheses in my own mind. It is, in fact, the only thing I ever wrote that was even once "not for publication." I write to make money, not to "express myself."

What the result will be I do not know. Perhaps the curious will go to Smithville—if they can find it. Perhaps psychologists will substantiate the facts and use them as a "modern example of mass-delusion" in their text books. And perhaps one certain person will read what I have written and laugh.

In closing, let me mention that the names are substitutes: Smithville, John Ellis, Elstrom, and the rest. Only Kesserich I have not changed. The name is so much a part of the man that I am unwilling to separate them. No matter. No one remembers Kesserich—except myself, and the people of Smithville.

George Kramer

CHAPTER 1

THE RIDDLE OF THE PEBBLES

Being a city dweller, I was astonished by the way the main cross street of Smithville, California, ended suddenly in the desert. I suppose that back in New York I had unconsciously thought of streets as going on forever; if they did end it would be at an apartment building or a river. But this one led to an ocean of sand and sage and then stopped. It was as if it said:

"Go through the desert in what direction you will; there are an infinite number of directions in the desert. But watch your step, for I am done with you. I have done my work in leading you there."

It reminded me of something that Kesserich had once said:

"If we humans ever gained the power to move in a fourth dimension, our former life in three would seem as cramping as being in a narrow tunnel."

The very immensity of the desert impressed me more than I had expected. Being on the edge of the little town of Smithville seemed to me like being on the boundary between the finite and the fearful infinite. And that idea too made me think of Kesserich.

It was only natural that I should be thinking of him, for I was on my way to pay him a visit. Daniel Kesserich, my college roommate, whom I had not seen for ten years.

On a rise half a mile ahead I could see the small, white house the hotel clerk had described to me.

"You'll find him there all right, I guess," he had said. "I haven't seen him for weeks, but then none of us sees a great deal of Mister Kesserich."

That was just what you always heard of Kesserich. Love of isolation was the seal he had set on his whole life. The only connection his very house had with the town was a couple of heavily insulated wires supported by a series of short, thick poles. I idly marveled at the size of the wires.

Three of us had been roommates, three of us had become fast friends: Daniel Kesserich, John Ellis, and myself, George Kramer. Then, as happens after college days, circumstances took them out of my life. John Ellis had come to this little California town to wed Mary Andrews, ward of a prominent local fruit grower, and to set up a medical practice. Mary Andrews had been our fellow student, come to far-off New York in the face of her guardian's objections. She had some money of her own. All three of us had liked her well.

Kesserich had come out to Smithville with the Ellises

and finally made his home there, where the clear, quiet air did not interfere with his star-gazing, his experiments, and his crystalline theory-spinning. I had taken my chance in New York and finally achieved some minor success as a writer. For ten years we had not seen one another; our letters had become fewer and fewer, finally ceased altogether. Friendship there still was, but inactive.

Only a month before I had chanced to look through the letters Kesserich had sent me during the first years. They seemed like a continuation of the nocturnal discussions we had at college and I felt myself caught by the old enthusiasm. How daringly young imaginations rip through the more speculative of scientific notions, especially those eternal riddles of space and time! There was the desert again! Kept one's mind coming back to the problem of the infinite.

Anyway, Kesserich had been a most astute critic in these matters. Strains of an old argument floated through my mind, one he repeated so often that we called it "the dirge."

"I wonder if all the people who talk so glibly of time-traveling have understood what it means: namely, that past and future ages are just as real as the present. Else there would be no places to travel to. And then what keeps us from time-traveling? Only the human mind, the human consciousness, which is bound down to one tiny bit of time, the present moment. But if we could ever get outside the present moment, we would see the world in four dimensions, the fourth being time. We would see *ourselves,* stretching out in a continuous line from the cradle to the grave. . . ."

I stopped to wonder what effect the desert had on Kesserich; the desert, a gigantic incubator for strange ideas.

It was John Ellis's letter that had brought me out west. It had told of the death of his wife, Mary. One of those sudden, purely accidental deaths that are therefore doubly heart-rending. "If she had only heard (I quote the letter) that her former guardian was trying out a new poisonous spray that did not stain the fruit or leave any visible sign. If that hired man hadn't forgotten, with murderous, damnable stupidity, to put up the written warning. If she hadn't happened to wander over there that fatal afternoon. If she hadn't happened to eat that particular orange off that particular tree . . ."

I could see in every line John's inability to cope with this sudden stroke of fate. Despite his choice of profession he was a high-strung, sensitive man. His being a doctor probably only made the tragedy hit him the harder. Between the lines I could read his need of companionship. As I had been planning a vacation for some time his letter decided me on Smithville. It was not purely an act of sympathy on my part; if bored or pained I could always go elsewhere; for years I'd wanted to see the west.

I was visiting Kesserich first to find out how the land lay

and what changes had taken place in John so that I'd know how best to approach him. Ten years is a long time.

By now I had come to the squat, white house. A little path lead to the door, strangely hedged on both sides by a wall of cactus and sage. I walked up it, raised my hand to knock out the familiar four and two raps that had been our signal at college . . . and hesitated. Old friendships are queer things. For the first time I began to wonder just how much Kesserich had changed. I might find that the old bond was no longer between us. The way to Kesserich's friendship and confidence was narrow, as narrow as the way between the two hedges where I now stood.

And, as I hesitated, the thing happened. I felt something push up beneath my foot. Moving away and looking down, I saw a tiny fragment of red sandstone. Just a tiny fragment, and there was a small pile of them at one side of the door—but I had not moved as I stood before the door and it had not been there when I had set my foot down, or else I would have felt it sooner. Or would I?

As I stared downward I heard a tiny noise behind me. I spun round; no one there; only, on the ground, lay another fragment of red sandstone. Had it been there before? I shivered. Small events like this, minute infractions of natural law, are always the most eerie.

Then, before my very eyes, a third red stone appeared several feet farther down the path. Appeared, I say. It was not thrown; it was not pushed up from under the ground. It just appeared. With trembling, cautious hand I picked it up; there seemed to be nothing unusual about it. And, as I inspected it dubiously, a fourth stone appeared farther on.

If I had stopped to puzzle over the business I might have become completely unnerved, but the regular way in which the pebbles kept appearing fascinated me. Of contrasting color, they stood out like a trail across the desert floor. Trail? How laid and by whom and leading where? All else for the moment forgotten, I thought only of following it.

I found myself being led back at a moderate pace toward a different part of town than that from which I had come. Sometimes I had difficulty in sighting the next stone, and this difficulty was a blessing in that it kept me from pondering on the monstrousness of what was happening.

Finally the trail took me to an orchard fenced by light wire. As I hesitated in perplexity, another fragment appeared a few feet on the other side. I vaulted over and kept on. The task was more difficult now; the grass hid the tiny pebbles I was looking for. Once I lost the trail altogether. As I circled around trying to pick it up my glance fell upon a small patch of dried mud and, as I looked, the print of a shoe appeared in it; appeared—in the same way as had the fragments. Now, for the first time, extreme horror overtook me.

Was I following the spoor of an invisible man? With a hectic desperation born of fear I dashed forward, my arms blindly groping for something tangible that I might grapple with. But I found nothing.

Then I examined the footprint. It was not new; it looked several days old. How could a distinct footprint in dried mud be anything but old? I asked myself, holding my dizzy head in my hands. Then, with a slight, hysterical laugh I noticed a red pebble a little farther on. My breath coming fast and my heart pounding, I was drawn forward.

The trail finally stopped at one of the orange trees; at least I could not find any continuation. Here the sod was trampled and there were many footprints, but none of them *appeared,* at least while I was watching. I wandered about, but could see nothing farther that was unusual. My fear was disappearing and in its place came an intellectual puzzlement like to nothing I have ever felt before. And then came a new fear: Was I insane? Were these stones hallucinations? What else could they be? I picked one of them up, half expecting it to melt away at my touch. Yet it was as maddeningly real and ordinary as only a bit of rock can be.

But had I really seen it appear? Did the hallucination lie there? I returned for a last look to the tree where the trail ended. A bit of white cloth was laying on the ground—I was certain that it had not been there before, yet . . . I picked it up. It was a handkerchief. On one corner were the initials J.E.

John Ellis!

The name came into my mind like a bullet. His wife accidentally poisoned by fruit from "that particular tree." Was this that tree? A new note, a gruesome one, was added to the riddle against which my mind futilely beat. I stood stupidly still, holding the bit of cloth in my hand.

Then I thought of Kesserich. This was just the sort of mystery that he had always wanted to come up against. Perhaps he could help explain things. Not that I thought they could be explained, but I had to talk to someone, someone who would not laugh or call the police to take me in charge as a lunatic. At a half run I doubled back toward his house, through the orchard, over the fence, past the graveyard that stood nearby, and on. As I ran I hardly thought of the fact that the trail had started at Kesserich's, or wondered what that might mean.

When I was about a hundred yards from the house came the climax of mysteries. There was a tremendous explosion; the shock of the sudden noise made me reel. When I looked up, the squat, white house had disappeared; in its place were two shaking walls and a wide scattering of fragments. I looked dumbfoundedly at the fat ball of smoke, the way it was beginning to roll away as unconcernedly as a little touring car that was chugging along almost a mile away across the desert . . .

Then I hurried ahead to search the ruins. After five minutes or so I was joined in this task by the members of the local fire department and other people who came speeding or running from the town.

We found clothing, bits of furniture, fragments of scientific apparatus, including an unbelievable quantity of copper wire. But of human remains, there was no trace.

"Guess he was out of town, boys," said the chief. "Any of you can puzzle out what might have caused it, 'cept a bomb? Well, I can't either."

"We all know Mister Kesserich sometimes used enough electricity to darken all the lights in the town," said an old man. "You can't do that and not get danger."

Others nodded darkly. Some small-town people never do seem to get really modernized. Underneath and without knowing it, they remain superstitious witch-fearers and witch-burners.

Perhaps it was because I was thinking of this that I surreptitiously pocketed a charred notebook I happened to find among the fragments of stucco. If I gave it to the fire captain or the chief of police, I thought, there'd be small chance of my ever glimpsing the contents, and besides, I somehow felt—it was the sort of thing you'd classify as a premonition—that I was going to have a hard time learning anything about Kesserich and every pertinent fragment would be valuable. However, at the time this was just a feeling.

It may seem rather strange that of all the searchers I alone should have discovered anything that promised information and it is indeed true that coincidence seemed to stalk me at Smithville. But I believe I was the only one that searched the ruins with any imagination and—as for the coincidence—well, it is only too often a name for unnoticed (I hardly say supernatural) forces.

Dusk with its desert chill found me mechanically making my way back to the hotel in which I now intended to take a room. Several days later I learned that the chief of police had seriously suspected me of being "the bomb thrower." He was apparently satisfied of my innocence by the casually extracted testimony of the hotel clerk and others. At least I was not arrested.

Upon reaching the hotel I remembered to inquire about the location of John Ellis's residence. I was told by the clerk that he had temporarily left town two days before. This was rumor insofar as I could find no one who had seen Ellis leaving town. Next morning the post office was unable to give me any forwarding address.

After supper I retired to my room to examine the notebook

I had discovered. I was immediately struck by a detail I should have noticed in the afternoon: the book was charred—something an explosion could hardly explain. The implication was obvious: the book had been burned previously—probably by Kesserich, for it was in his script—possibly by another. But not completely burned. True, a great sheaf of early pages was completely missing; either it had been torn out or else twisted so that it had been burned through. However, a few pages at the back were comparatively whole; either they had been overlooked or their destruction had not been imperative. These I will now copy down.

CHAPTER 2

REMAINS OF A NOTEBOOK

. . . There being this time no noticeable distortion. Strange that I didn't think of using morphine the first time; then there would have been none of those amazing distortions. (Still, what is as convincing as a distortion of reality?) But what drugs have accomplished intellect can duplicate. I need only assure myself of the reliability of the time-control. Make it automatic! Why not? Operating at regular, spaced intervals.

What will I find on the other side? But why speculate or, rather, why write down speculations? Written words never could keep up with my brain.

April 23. What can I write? Now that it is over, or rather begun. How to describe the indescribable? Not in words but possibly in metaphorical hints. There must be some way to keep a link between the two worlds—no, between the real world and its cross-section. It is like, my dear Ellis: standing between two mirrors and seeing oneself reflected back and forth between the two. Endlessly. A series of images stretching out to infinity, becoming smaller and smaller, vaguer and vaguer, until invisible or indistinguishable.

April 27. Imagine a man who had lived all his life in a tunnel, a tunnel so narrow that the sides forever pressed upon his shoulders. Never could get away from their touch. Came to think that the sides of the tunnel were as inevitable a part of his existence as the air he breathed, the blood that coursed through his body . . .

Then imagine him a grown man, reaching an exit somehow, getting out into the open. Seeing everything expand around him. It would be a miracle to him. Almost kill him. Like taking the ground out from under a man's feet. For he'd be as used to the side walls as any man is today to that ground under his feet; more used. I, Kesserich the poet, say so. Kesserich the Multiple knows. "If I should take the wings of the morning and fly to the uttermost parts of the earth . . ." But I've done just that, Ellis, just that. O yes, Mr. Ellis, o yes.

Experimental conversations between John Ellis, the unenlightened, and Daniel Kesserich, the first multiple man (insert this title back to the beginning of the entry for April 23).

May 6. However.

Being a judgment upon one Daniel Kesserich's gift to mankind by his only peer, Himself:

DANGERS:	BENEFITS:

Dangers
Benefits

CHAPTER 3

SMALL TALK

With this strangely judicial, almost satirical beginning of an inventory, the entries in the diary—to give it a name—seemed to end. In spite of the book's damaged condition I was fairly sure of this because the words "Dangers" and "Benefits" headed an empty page; none of the intended entries in the two columns had been made. Further, "Benefits" ended in a savage flourish that scratched an inky line through the paper and onto the page underneath.

There would be no point in my denying that the reading of this scribbled statement left me in a distinctly uneasy frame of mind. It is true that it was incomplete and in no real sense intelligible. True that its incomprehensible fantasizing and bizarre sardonicness was characteristic of Kesserich's strange humor. True, in fact and to avoid further suppressing my chief reaction, it seemed definitely, screamingly, to hint at a serious derangement in the mind of my college friend.

Insanity, yes! But that was just what bothered me. Yesterday it might have offered me an easy explanation of

Kesserich's disappearance and the destruction of his domicile. But not today, not after . . . Insanity! I had myself seen strange things, things which, if they came in sufficient number, would make me scribble just such statements, wild, mad . . .

Madness? Can it sometimes be caught like a disease? From friend or passerby? From patting the head of a child or talking to a hotel clerk? Like a disease, does it linger in certain localities, dormant, waiting? Could I . . .

You can easily see where my thoughts led me that night. However, the further I went in the realm of morbid fancy the more sure I became of my own soundness, the more I became sure that I had stumbled upon something that was not hallucination.

Had Kesserich? Careful perusal of his document showed that it made especial reference to two things: drugs, and states of mind not ordinarily to be found in man. This suggested to me mysticism, occult trances, yogis, fakirs . . . with a start I remembered that these were subjects in which Kesserich had once shown something more than a passing interest. Eagerly I reread the smoke-yellowed fragments, noting with a nod that the "time-control" mentioned might refer to some device for awakening a man from a trance that might have dangerous consequences if indefinitely prolonged. Only what could he then mean by "distortions" and how could the use of morphine have an effect on such distortions, whatever they might be? Reluctantly I had to admit that I had not yet enough material in my hands to make sure that my idea of "drug experiments" was more than a promising hypothesis.

The course of action I decided upon was the obvious one. I would at least stay on for a while. I was on vacation and I was determined to get to the bottom of the mystery I had walked into. By this time I was convinced of my own sanity and beginning to doubt the sanity of nature.

So next morning I set out on a conscientious campaign of investigation. I talked freely to whomever I could, slipping in cautiously worded questions. I looked through the files of the local newspaper. In one a couple of days old I found the following article:

Mrs. Olga Peterson was treated by Dr. John Ellis for a superficial head injury. She claims that while walking along Dory Lane a stone came through the air and struck her. It is thought to be the work of mischievous boys. We urge parents to remind their children of the criminal element in such pranks.

Mrs. Peterson claims that she saw no one and that if there had been anyone near enough to throw the stone she would have seen them. Naturally this contention that "the stone just came through the air from nowhere" is not to be taken seriously; Mrs. Peterson does not realize that it is the ideal of every small boy to throw accurately over long distances.

Afterwards I examined the scene of this occurrence myself. As I half expected, half feared, it was just beyond the orchard I had been led to the day before. From the spot where Mrs. Peterson had been struck to the nearest place of concealment in the orchard was approximately four hundred feet.

Returning from the newspaper office I noticed that something was going on at the courthouse, dropped in, and found that James Totten, hired hand, was being tried for criminal negligence in the matter of the death of the wife of Dr. Ellis. The place was packed. Totten was on the stand. Under a fire of biting questions he was maintaining his innocence.

"Why, Mister Lawyer, I distinctly remember that Mr. Elstrom never told me nothin' special about puttin' up a sign on the tree where I'd used the new spray. Course I was careful myself, but I never even remembers him sayin' anything about its bein' 'specially poisonous, and—"

At this moment a thin, sour-faced, middle-aged man jumped up and cut in with, "He lies! I distinctly told him to be very careful and to put up a warning, some kind of a warning. I got a weak heart and I won't have him contradicting me! He's only trying to squirm out from—"

There was a flurry of excitement in the audience. The judge rapped for order. The sour-faced man glared around for a moment and then sat down. I afterwards verified my guess that he was Elstrom, Mary Ellis's former guardian. He, and the whole affair for that matter, created a distinctly disagreeable sensation in my mind. I remembered a phrase in the letter I had gotten from Ellis: "And I can't help being bitter toward Elstrom. It was his business to see that all precautions were used when the new spray was being tested. And I can't keep myself from thinking that he was secretly delighted when Mary died. He wanted her for himself, always did. Couldn't bear the sight of me—or of Mary, after she married me. These are nasty and unfounded notions of mine, but it's just that sort of thing that I can't keep out of my mind now."

I left the courtroom. The next day I read that Totten had been acquitted on the grounds of insufficient evidence. A couple of days later he left town. He had no chance of getting a local job, I suppose. I didn't get to talk to him.

And still I found myself just as far as ever from the beginning of a solution of the mystery. I did find out that the orange tree that the trail had led me to had been the one from which Mary had eaten the poisoned fruit. That tied things together but did not make them any clearer. What invisible thing would lay a pebble trail to the tree that everyone knew about? What . . . but why continue with speculations that only end with making one superstitious?

My attempts to get in touch with John Ellis and Daniel Kesserich ended in failure.

I read everything I could find concerning the circumstances surrounding the death of Mary Ellis. Without telling anyone, she had come over to spend an afternoon reading in the pleasant shade of the orchard trees. She had been found lying dead near the new-sprayed tree, a half-eaten orange and her book beside her. Evidently death had overtaken her unexpectedly.

All this told me little.

However, when I interviewed the slightly bruised Mrs. Peterson, she told me that the small rock that had struck her had been a fragment of red sandstone.

CHAPTER 4

TEMPORARY INTERRUPTION OF A CHURCH SERVICE

I spent the next two days in wandering about the town. I seemed to have exhausted all the obvious and reasonable sources of information. Yet there was something in the atmosphere of the town that hinted at clues just beyond my reach. It seemed to have something to do with the people. A furtive and fearful unrest was the nearest I could come to describing it. There were some definite incidents that seemed to hook up with it but, without the atmosphere, I'd hardly have noticed them.

My second evening in Smithville I passed a little church at dusk. The doors were open and, as I lingered before them, I heard the subdued intonations of the minister's voice as he announced and commenced to read the lesson from the Old Testament. About halfway through he was interrupted by a muffled shriek from one of the women in the congregation, who pushed her way from her pew and ran down the aisle toward me as though the devil himself were at her heels. She was followed and stopped by a man, evidently her husband,

and by two other women who looked equally fearful, although they managed not to scurry. None of them returned to the church.

I found that out because I listened to the rest of the service, hesitatingly resumed, from a seat in the dimly lighted last row. All the way through I got an impression of tension from the people before me. Perhaps it was the way some of them seemed to crouch in their seats, all the while spying about furtively—even in prayer. And there was occasionally just the suggestion of a shudder in the minister's voice.

When the service was over the members of the congregation didn't lose any time in getting away, so I had no trouble in being the last one out and in engaging the minister in conversation after he had shook my hand at the door. He was a young man, cultivated, likely new to the town. His hair was dark; his face, thin. His name was Ferguson. When I spoke of the hysterical behavior of the woman he gave me a curious look.

"It was strange," he agreed. "Everyone's been jumpy today. I noticed it at choir practice too. And don't think that sort of concerted feeling doesn't affect even me. If I were a strict fundamentalist, sir—which I'm not—I'd be inclined to say that the creatures that flew by night in the ruins of Babylon had swooped down here. I mention that, figuratively of course, because it describes the feeling well."

"The woman's fright," I pressed, "couldn't just possibly have had something to do with what you were reading?"

"Ah . . . no. I hardly think so. It was just, let me see, the . . . the thirty-seventh chapter of the book of the prophet Ezekiel. I've used it quite often. Ah . . . well . . . by the by, you're a visitor in Smithville, aren't you, sir?"

"Why, yes," I admitted, "A friend of Dr. Ellis's—"

My companion visibly started but immediately recovered himself; what seemed to be a look of puzzlement was on his face.

"Was he a member of your congregation?" I quickly asked.

"Why, yes . . . yes . . . I conducted the service at his wife's funeral."

I could not be sure in the half darkness, but when I parted from him a little later under the door light, I thought his face had paled.

Before I went to bed that night I took up from my dresser the inevitable Gideon Bible and read through the chapter the minister had mentioned, lingering over certain passages: ". . . and set me down in the midst of the valley which was full of bones . . . and, lo, they were very dry . . . so I prophesied as I was commanded: and, as I prophesied, there was a noise, and behold a shaking, and the bones came together, bone to his bone."

And what was it that Ferguson had said about "creatures that flew by night in the ruins of Babylon?"

CHAPTER 5

EVENTS CONNECTED WITH A BURIAL

Another happening that helped to keep my interest on edge—and it hardly needed helping—was even more cryptic. I was passing down the main street when a woman rushed out of a door, a man holding on to her hand and expostulating with her.

"No, Mr. Posten!" she said wildly, "I'm going to tell them as should know. I got to—"

"Now, now, Miss Harkness," he argued in a guarded voice that was at once persuasive and compelling. "You shan't do anything of the sort. You're just nervous and all you'll do is cause a lot of excitement. And you know as well as I do that your notion is perfectly ridiculous. Come on, now, before more people see you, and talk it all over with Mrs. Simmons. She knows as well as I do how this work can get on a person's nerves. Come on, now."

With a doubtful look she allowed herself to be led back inside.

It was then that I noticed the sign over the door; it read: "Posten and Sons' Funeral Parlor."

But from the first something in my mind had connected this little incident with what had happened at the church. That something was the look on the face of the frightened woman. And all the while I had the feeling that other little things were happening around me that I just missed getting in on.

So I kept on wandering. Morning of the third day found me on the grounds of the Smithville Perpetual Nest Cemetery. I chanced upon the sexton, a dour old man, and asked him to direct me to the grave of Mary Ellis. He started guiltily at the name—I was getting used to that reaction—and pointed out the way, following me up with obviously furtive glances.

The grave was partly shaded by two unhealthy eucalyptus trees. The sodded rectangle of ground was already yellowing—hardly in accord with the promises of "Perpetual Care," I thought. Kneeling up close in the poor light I read all of the inscription on the headstone; then my eyes wandered down to the flat stone marking the foot. Blocked out in severe lettering on its surface I read the name "Mary." I started to look away but found my glance turned back to it. There was something queer about it, something twisted . . . suddenly I realized what it was.

I could see the letters where I stood and I was standing at the head of the grave! All footstones I had ever seen were

POSTON and Sons'
Funeral Parlor

made to be read from the opposite direction. Here was more evidence of the carelessness of the cemetery attendants! I reached down to turn the stone, hesitated, and rose, calling to the sexton.

He seemed to have difficulty in understanding me.

"What is it?" he shouted.

"Something wrong here," I sent back rather brusquely.

He dropped the edger with which he had been working on a path and came hurrying.

"I knowed it, I knowed it," he said breathlessly as he drew up. "For two days I been worrying. I felt in my bones that something was wrong."

"What did you know? What something?" I questioned sharply.

"O, things I keep rememberin'," he answered vaguely and again I caught the guilty glance.

"Well," I said, "what's happened here is that the foot-stone's been put in wrong." He stared at me as though he had expected me to say something entirely different.

"Put in wrong," I repeated. "Upside down. It faces the wrong way."

He looked at the stone. His eyes squinted and then opened wide.

"Why," he said, "I put that there stone in myself. I ain't never made any mistakes like that."

"And look at the condition of the grass," I went on bitingly.

At my words the sexton began to tremble. He knelt and pulled at a piece of sodding. It came up without difficulty. The face he raised to mine was full of fear, fear and a dawning suspicion.

"Come on, mister," he said, "we got to go to the authorities about this.

"Why?" I questioned, half expecting the answer that came.

"Somebody's been into the grave. And I think I know who."

I cannot rid my mind of the dreamlike quality of the events that followed. People entered and moved through them as though hypnotized.

Sexton Eldredge and I first visited Hopkins, the owner of the cemetery. We went with him to the police.

"But surely," I said, "there's no such thing as grave robbing today?"

He shook his head. "There's sometimes jewelry to be gone after; and there's madmen and . . . well, I know something's wrong here. Know it."

I expected the chief of police to be skeptical, but he, too, was strangely impressed with my discovery.

"Call Dr. Kingsbury," he directed his subordinate, explaining to me, "He's the man that wrote out Mrs. Ellis's death certificate, I bet."

Then, without explaining why in the world it was necessary that the doctor be called, he turned to the sexton with an "Eldredge, what else do you know about this?"

Eldredge quickly looked at us all, took a deep breath, and said, "I never thought nothing of it at the time, but this is what happened. About five nights ago"—that would be about two days before I arrived—"I'm goin' my last round (that's just after dark) and I sees Dr. Ellis standin' near his wife's grave. And I ain't surprised, only sorry for him the way he's been hit by his wife's death. Well, he sorta smiles at me, quick like, and tells me he'll be out before I finish up. Then I go on with my round. Come to think of it though, his voice was sorta excited, quick like—if you get what I mean. Funny, how I remember.

"Anyway, whiles later I'm finishin' up and, just as I'm gettin' near the gate, I hears it close, softly like. And the next second I get a big start 'cause I think I see somebody slippin' into the shrubbery—*inside* the gate, mind you. Well, I take my flash and shoot it around but I don't see nothin' more. So I go off home, thinkin' all the time I'd just heard Dr. Ellis shuttin' the gate as he went off."

"Why didn't you report to me about what you saw?" came sharply from Hopkins.

"Well, sir, of course you see I just thought I'd had a fit of nerves. Just like anybody's apt to get at night. Sure, I never figured I'd saw anything real. I figured I'd just seen a shadow . . . then."

"What was this person you thought you saw like?" questioned the chief.

"Couldn't say. If 'twas a man he was dressed in black; a long black coat. Somehow he seems familiar but there's no more I can say about it."

"Familiar?"

"Yes sir, but I can't say how."

"What did you mean when you said 'if it was a man'?"

Eldredge hesitated a moment and then muttered something unconvincing about how "it mighta been a woman."

In this short time quite a few people had gathered in and in front of the police station. I know news spreads rapidly in small towns but here it must have spread like wildfire through a dry field. And sibilant—like fire through corn—rustled their whispers, the whispers of the gathering crowd. The subtle noise grew in volume, then suddenly ceased. Those out in front of the station craned their necks down the street whence there came a more insistent voice, high, feminine, and hysterical. A doctor pushed his way through the crowd, followed by the woman I had seen the day before in front of the undertaker's parlor. There was a look in her eyes compound of terror and triumph. Her lips were tight now; she was confidently biding her time, though why or for what I could not imagine. The medical man was plainly rattled.

"Dr. Kingsbury," boomed the chief, "there has come to my attention evidence that the grave of Mrs. John Ellis has been disturbed and possibly entered. Now . . ."

He paused.

"That's most unfortunate," Kingsbury replied, shifting nervously, "but I fail to see how it concerns me."

"Well," said the chief slowly, "you wrote out her death certificate, didn't you?"

"Yes sir, Dr. Ellis and I both examined her. But I still fail to see why you sent for me."

The chief scratched his head. It was obvious that he was painfully bewildered. His behavior struck in my memory a chord I could not interpret. Why he had made such a stupid mistake as to send for a doctor I could not imagine.

Then the woman from the undertaker's, Miss Harkness, took a hand in the game.

"Go on," she hissed at Kingsbury, "tell them what you know, you coward."

"Chief," he said quickly, "Miss Harkness started to

scream at me in the street and followed me all the way over here. I can't imagine what she's so excited about. I—"

"You can't, can't you?" she cut in with loud sarcasm. "O no, none of you know a thing! O, no! But deep down in your hearts you know, all of you. And you're scared to death on account of what you've done. And won't admit it. No. But that won't help you because I'm going to tell you all. Mary Ellis wasn't embalmed! I know. I helped to wash her up. Mary Ellis was buried alive!"

The hush was intense.

Upon every face was a look of wonder, but—and this was the amazing thing—not so much wonder as comprehension. It was just as Miss Harkness had said; they looked as if they'd known it all "deep in their hearts." They looked guilty. But, further, they looked exactly as though they'd just become certain of something they had only unconsciously known before.

All that could be heard for a moment was the chalk-pale doctor weakly mumbling something about "ridiculous." Then the chief reacted.

"Come on, Kingsbury," he shouted. "Eldredge, get a couple of shovels as we go. We're going to exhume that grave!"

And they rushed off, the crowd following them to a man.

CHAPTER 6

CONSEQUENCES OF AN EXHUMATION

Slowly I stepped out of a corner into which I had been violently pushed during the scramble. Without thinking why I was doing what I was doing I shook my head, as if to clear my mind. It was just as if I'd witnessed a scene in an insane asylum and was now left, a discarded piece of sanity, alone.

No, not quite alone.

For, leaning back against the inward opened door, clutching the knob as though for support, a set look on a face that seemed focused on terror, was my acquaintance, the young minister Ferguson. I strode down toward him.

"Mr. Ferguson," I said simply, "I've seen some things. But I've never seen the police quite so helter-skelter. I've never seen a town gone so mad. Can you tell me what it is?"

He looked up at me slowly, got himself under control, and shook his head.

"You're an intellectual," I went on frankly. "You're a young man. You're fresh from a big city and a metropolitan seminary. And now you've seen all this. You have the power to look at it objectively. What do you make of it?"

"Well . . ." he faltered. "There's mass-psychology."

"To name it doesn't explain it," I insisted violently. "Mass-psychology? How? Why?"

"Yes . . . yes . . ." he agreed slowly. "But it's all so indefinite, so insubstantial."

"That's just it!" I fired back. "Indefinite, insubstantial—a sort of mass feeling, an epidemic of guilty faces and fearful eyes. But look how it affected men like the chief and Dr. Kingsbury. And look how they accepted Miss Harkness's hysterical, ridiculous assertions without asking her one question. And now—going off to exhume a grave without even going through the proper legal procedure. It's simply incomprehensible, don't you see?"

"O, I see well enough," he replied, a new note in his voice, a note strong and strange. "I've seen more than you're looking for, perhaps. For let me tell you, Mr. Kramer, I'm not myself immune to what you're pleased to call this 'epidemic.' When Miss Harkness spoke I actually found myself believing what she said: that Mary Ellis had been buried alive. And, worse, I seemed to remember looking at her face during the funeral and seeing color in her cheeks and a fluttering of her eyelids. It's horrible. I can't even now get the picture out of my mind."

"The power of suggestion . . ." I began.

"It's more real than that, Mr. Kramer."

"But you say you only just now get this delusion; that is, you *only just now* remembered all this about Mrs. Ellis."

"That's it," he nodded eagerly. "A couple of days ago the fear first came."

Like a germ, like a contagious disease, I thought.

"And at first," he went on, "I kept shoving it out of my mind. I guess I kept it pretty well under until Miss Harkness crystallized it for me. My God, I hardly suspected that the others had it too. What can it, can it be? It's like . . . yes, it's like coming out of a deep hypnotic trance. I've been a subject once or twice, you see, and I know."

Hypnosis! That was what I'd been trying to think of. And something else: post-hypnotic suggestion! That would explain such things as the chief of police stupidly sending for Dr. Kingsbury when there was no cause; it was as if he'd been told to do it by a master hypnotist. But then how to explain Miss Harkness, Eldredge, and the rest? How could so many be hypnotized by a mere man? Impossible. He would have to have powers undreamed of; the power of hypnotizing and suggesting from a distance, hypnotizing by telepathy. For a moment I was lost in a vision, the vision of a man sitting lonely in a lonely room, managing the people of Smithville like puppets, drawing them about sardonically by invisible mind-strings. . . . Suddenly I realized that thinking could wait. I broke the vision.

"Do you want to go on with me and see what they do at the grave?" I asked Ferguson.

He started to shake his head, then nodded. We walked fast. When we hit the street leading to the cemetery stragglers began to hurry past us, those who were late in getting the news and those who had farther to come—distraught yet silent folk. We glimpsed many scenes, caught many scraps of quick conversation. One thing sticks in my mind: a little boy dragging at his mother's hand and screaming out, "I didn't let her be buried alive! Honest I didn't!"

It is not good for children to be as terrified as that one was. There was something sick and sinking at the pit of my stomach.

"What was that rot about not embalming the body?" I asked Ferguson.

He shook his head. "Not rot, truth. Ellis wanted it that way." He jerked back at me.

The cemetery looked as if a full half of Smithville's citizens had been unceremoniously dumped into it from the sky. There was a good deal of whispering and some sobbing, but little loud talk and no screaming. There was a compulsive restraint, a tenseness, as if all of us had been scooped, breathless, into the palm of one man's hand. We arrived at what seemed to be a crisis, but then I suppose that everything that happened that day was of the nature of a crisis.

People were crowded close around Mary Ellis's grave, where a full half-dozen furious shovelers were getting in each other's way and making for delay.

"Go it faster!" yelled a distraught woman and then added ridiculously, "There's still time to save her!"

An old woman, clutching an ear trumpet in one hand and the chief of police's coat lapel in the other, was screaming at him:

"I tell you, on that selfsame night that the sexton says as there was prowlers, I saw somebody loitering near the gate. My house is right by and I'm always at the window. Well, that person I saw, and he didn't look good to me, that person was Mister Kesserich."

"Who?" said the chief, suddenly beginning to pay attention.

"Mister Kesserich!" The hag's answer was almost a howl. It turned Sexton Eldredge around like a shot.

"That's it!" his voice joined in the pandemonium. "That's who I thought I saw sneakin' around like a shadow after the gate was closed. Mister Kesserich! He done it!"

It seemed to me rather early to talk about anything having been done and I said as much to Ferguson, who kept close beside me. He nodded, but I could tell that his nod was merely an intellectual automatism.

There came a cry from one of the diggers that the coffin

top had been uncovered. The cemetery became silent save for the squeal of screws and the hard breathing from those who had been shouting or running about. Then, like an actor who had perfectly timed his entrance, Mr. Elstrom strode up to the crowd around the grave. I hardly recognized the little pursy man whom I had seen crabbing in the courtroom. Now he looked haunted. Haunted and frightened. But he forced his voice to take on a tone of command.

"See here," he bellowed, save for an occasional laryngitic squeak, "I'll have the lot of you clapped into jail. You too," he continued, pointing at the chief of police, who hardly heard him. "And stop this desecration at once! What do you mean by entering a grave without consent of next-of-kin or those that have the say? I'll take it to the state. I'll make you smart for it. Stop it, right now!"

He was interrupted, or answered, by the dull thump of wood on sod. Those around the grave looked down. I could almost see their trembling as they started back. The chief of police turned to Elstrom.

"Guess you'll allow we had right," he said in a low voice. "We knew what was what. The casket's empty. Mary Ellis's body is gone."

The color drained from Elstrom's face. Making a little clucking noise in his throat he fell senseless to the ground.

CHAPTER 7

IN THE MINISTER'S STUDY

Ferguson's hand trembled as he lighted a cigarette. I could see that this annoyed him; he clenched both fists hard before settling himself in a chair that faced the comfortable one in which I was already ensconced. The light was restfully shaded. About us were books and a few small objects of art, inexpensive but tasteful.

"With all this excitement," I began abruptly, "we've got to keep what facts there are carefully organized. Now, as far as I can see, we're dealing with two separate strings of ideas, and it'll be a good thing to keep them separate. I'll take the simpler one first."

"You mean the disappearance of the body, the grave robbing?" put in Ferguson. Obviously he was as glad as I to have an intelligent person to talk things over with.

"Yes. Now there's evidence that Kesserich, yes, and John Ellis were around the cemetery after dark and after-hours five days—was it five?—yes, five days ago."

"But remember, Mr. Kramer, there's no precise evidence to show that was the night on which the body was stolen."

"Very true," I replied thoughtfully, "and we have only the word of an antique sexton and a deaf woman as to their presence, though I must admit I'm inclined to credit them. Their testimony sounded like something from the well of truth itself compared to some of the stuff we've heard responsible people saying today."

Ferguson shifted uncomfortably.

"Of course," he said, "it's inevitable that their suspicions should turn to Kesserich. You knew him at college, didn't you? I suppose he's just the usual independent scholar: eccentric, a recluse, but nothing more except perhaps a generous allotment of sardonic humor. I've been here almost two years and can't truthfully say that I've seen anything more. But the rumor! Especially during the last two months. If you hadn't already seen something of the people in this town you wouldn't believe me. I tell you their attitude toward Kesserich was that of a medieval serf toward a black magician, a puritan scullery girl toward a so-called witch. That is not an exaggeration."

"But what was the cause of this attitude?"

Ferguson shrugged his shoulders helplessly.

"Don't know," he said briefly. "Lonely life, language they couldn't understand. Can't guess further."

"O, he used to like to impress and frighten people even in the old days," I assured him. "You don't mean to tell me, though, that this afternoon was an average sample of Smithville behavior?"

Ferguson shook his head and smiled.

"No, certainly not. I'm afraid I was doing what we'd decided not to, that is, mix separate groups of facts and ideas. No, I must say there was nothing inexplicable in the rumors. Given a small town like this and a sardonic mystifier like your friend Kesserich and they can be explained."

"Well, then," I went on, "that leaves only one thing outstanding to speak against Ellis and Kesserich: the fact that they've disappeared. Disappeared would be too strong a word—for, after all, no one's even tried to get in touch with them—except for things like the blowing up of Kesserich's cottage. Does your reasoning let you see any further in this direction?"

The minister shook his head slowly. He was obviously surprised that I spoke out thus frankly against people I claimed were my friends. However, I thought it best; there was nothing to be gained by refusing to see points that were obvious to anyone.

"Then," I continued, "that brings us bang-up against the main business: this—well, I would call it insane if it weren't for what you told me in the police station—but, anyway, this impossible notion that seems to have struck half the people in Smithville, the notion that Mary Ellis was buried alive."

I paused but Ferguson remained silent, so I went on:

"Now, there was nothing secret about her burial, was there? And in a burial that isn't secret many people are involved, many see the body. Just how could anything happen? I know she wasn't embalmed, but that is often the case, as you are well aware. Personally, I can understand the reasons that motivated Dr. Ellis there. I've known him fairly well. Of course, we've all heard stories of people being buried while in cataleptic trance, but this wasn't catalepsy—it was poison. And then there's the crucial point that the idea that Mary Ellis was buried alive sprang up in people's minds almost a week *after* her funeral. Why in the world that interval before the epidemic of guilt? God, almost like the incubation period of a germ! But surely that *interval* proves that the whole thing must be some strange and unusual mass-delusion. You yourself surely don't think there could be anything real behind it? It's absurd to think of a secret cult having as members half the citizens in this town, a cult devoted to burying its initiates or its enemies alive."

Ferguson ran his finger around inside his collar and smiled in an unconvincing fashion.

"Surely not," he answered, "even though we are near the hotbed of cults and ignorant faddish religions—I mean Hollywood. No, it must be, as you say, a mass delusion, though I am hard put to admit it, for that means I am one of those

NOR LIE IN DEATH
FOREVER

suffering . . . er . . . from the . . . mental epidemic."

I looked at him, puzzled.

"You told me as much in the police station," I said. "But do you really mean that you actually think that the woman whose funeral service you preached was buried alive? Don't you mean that you sympathize with the delusion in others and that you've been imagining what it would be like if you had it yourself?"

"Hardly, hardly, though it's difficult for me to admit it. It's this way: for the past two or three days I've found my mind full of disturbing pictures—Mrs. Ellis lying in the coffin with color in her cheeks under the undertaker's rouge and with her lips moving a little, feebly. Things like that. But so strong that they almost completely drown out my memories of what actually happened. Can it be that everyone in this town is suffering from a silly, morbid obsession? Why, it is as if some demon of the upper air had opened our brains and scattered in seeds of unrest. For let me tell you that the thing grows, just as plants sprout from seeds. I'll wager that at this very moment many people of Smithville are sitting at home, shivering, wondering if they're going mad. It's only because I can see things like that and talk over the matter with you that even I am beginning to get a grip on myself. You're outside all this; you can't know how terrible it is to have one's very memory tampered with."

I shook my head hopelessly.

"You mentioned hypnotism, pastor, didn't you?" I ventured at random. "But . . . O, I admit there was something very reminiscent of the hypnotized in the people I saw this afternoon. But that can't mean anything very obvious, can it, like a mastermind working on this whole town? That would be silly. How could he operate? What could his methods be?"

Just then there came a subdued rapping at the door opening on the side of the house where the church stood. Ferguson opened it and I heard a man say something about, "wanting him, please, to come and read the litany."

Ferguson made me excuses as he fumbled in the closet for his cassock; he murmured something about "having to give consolation at all times and for all causes."

For a moment my heart stood still, my mind held by a vision of a pale-faced man in black holding the minds of his congregation by the monotony of ritual, by the *hypnotic* quality of his voice. . . .

Ferguson stood before me, thin and stiff in his black cassock. With a quick laugh I got up.

As I passed the open doors of the church a little later, after taking leave of the warm study, I heard the voices of the congregation, hoarse, heartfelt, and a trifle wild:

"God have mercy upon us."

"Christ have mercy upon us."

CHAPTER 8

INMATES OF AN EMPTY HOUSE

As usual the streets were dark and empty but only a few of the houses were lighted up, and these brilliantly, which was unusual. People had chosen this night to go visiting, to band together; probably the franker ones admitted that the force was fear. Passing Elstrom's place I noticed him standing on the porch with three men, one of whom seemed to be trying to persuade him to go in and to bed.

"No!" I caught from Elstrom, as his voice rose vindictively. "I won't stay out of this. He's scared . . . trying to save his own neck . . . I know it . . . used a different poison . . . my own dear little girl, God rest her . . . possibility of an autopsy . . . where's he gone? . . . have any idea . . ."

His voice sank and I heard no more. The other men seemed now to be listening to him intently. I moved on. The town was in a distraught and menacing mood. Thus, I thought, must Paris have seemed before the revolution and Jerusalem the night before the resurrection, Jerusalem . . . it reminded me of the ministry and of Ferguson, the one man in a position to—I laughed shortly—at myself. What rot?

Was it rot?

My thought roamed aimlessly around the problem of Smithville. With almost a start I realized that I hadn't told Ferguson of my experience with the appearing pebbles. I laughed again, shortly. Who was I to criticize people for their mass obsessions? When all the time I myself was hiding my own hallucinations for fear, unconscious or otherwise, of ridicule—or worse. Or worse. With a start I realized, realized fully for the first time, how easily an active imagination could connect me, George Kramer, with the suggestive things that had been happening. I had been the first one to reach the exploded house. I had been the one to call attention to Mary Ellis's grave. I was known to be a friend of Ellis and Kesserich. All this was innocent but to an irrational crowd, looking for a scapegoat . . . ? To my jangled nerves it seemed that Smithville, in a gesture of menace, drew back from me, crouching in the darkness.

John Ellis's house loomed up on my right, angular, black, and mysterious. Several times before, my walks had carried me past it and its double garage, but this time I was in a mood to test all eventualities, however improbable. I walked up quickly to the door and impulsively rapped out our old college signal: four, two.

Almost before I was finished and to my great surprise the

door shot open; there was a muffled exclamation and the door began to slam to, was stopped.

"Kesser-, Kramer, aren't you?" in nervous tones I recognized as those of John Ellis!

I nodded and he motioned me in, immediately locking the door. I hardly knew what to think, tensed myself for surprises.

"Thought you were Kesserich," he muttered, then changed his tone. "I didn't know you were out here; never expected to see you."

We stood in darkness. He made no move to turn on lights.

"Of course, there was your letter," I murmured tentatively.

"Ah, yes." And then abruptly, almost ferociously, "You've been out here several days? You've seen things? The cemetery this afternoon and all that?"

I intimated that I had. I didn't say much. I was realizing very rapidly that I was suspicious and even afraid of my old friend. However, I did ask him how he had learned all about the happenings of the afternoon.

"Simple," he replied shortly. "Country telephones. You can listen in on everything."

Suddenly he stood very still, listening.

"Sit down, won't you?" he resumed after a moment.

I complied. He paced up and down; I caught him damning Kesserich in undertones. Then he broke off and raced up the stair. A few moments later he came down, slowly.

My own thoughts at the time? Squirming things that touched the possibilities of insanity, murder, affection wrought to the pitch of ghoulery . . . they were interrupted and at the same time reintensified by my first real glimpse of Ellis's face, momentarily spotted by a beam of night light from a window. It was very haggard but there burned in it instead of grief an excitement and a joy that I definitely did not like. I continued to sit tight, leashing my questions.

"Kramer," he said deliberately, breaking off his pacing close to my chair and looking down at me, "I've thought of you as the one person in the world besides Kesserich to whom I could narrate and justify this business, and Kesserich is gone God knows where. And now that you, Kramer, are here I realize how utterly ridiculous it would be even to make the attempt."

His voice was heavy with world-irony.

Silently invoking friendship and besting fear I risked an encouragement. I told him of my experience with the appearing pebbles. There was a moment's pause, magnified by the darkness, and then from Ellis a little amused snort that made my hair rise.

"The luck of it," he muttered, "the uncanny, sumptuous luck of it, that such a thing should happen to you of all people. You deserve the story. Here it is."

The next chapter is a faithful attempt to reproduce what he told me, up to the point at which he was strangely interrupted.

CHAPTER 9

SPECULATIONS OF KESSERICH

(THE STATEMENT OF DR. JOHN ELLIS)

Any way you look at it, the story has to begin with Kesserich. You remember the discussions we used to have at college, the ones about space and time—and other things? But of course you would. Come to think of it, I believe you were more truly interested in them than I was. Perhaps that was the subtle reason for Kesserich's coming out here to live. He knew he'd always have me to talk to and he also knew that I wouldn't, well, bother him with too many comments, and suggestions, and criticisms. He's a queer chap, that way. He doesn't like friends to get too close to his inner thoughts. You've seen that in him too, I'm sure. Strange, he could have gotten for himself the most brilliant of intellectual associates, and yet he preferred a couple of people—you and me—who I guess I can safely say aren't any more than average, at least in his line. Who knows but that even then he faintly saw what was coming, felt somehow compelled to keep aloof from men . . . it's hard to say.

But he couldn't have seen all that was coming . . . you won't believe . . .

Well, anyway I was always willing to listen to him; I liked the man tremendously and his imagination fascinated me—those being my callow days, when I fancied myself as being something of a psychologist. Every week I would manage to find a few hours that weren't taken up with my practice or with Mary and I'd go over and listen to Kesserich's latest plan for overcoming the limitations of the human mind. He'd never come to visit me; I think he felt that Mary had taken a dislike to him for some reason. Perhaps she had; it was difficult not to misunderstand him.

Well, one evening that I drove out to his little cottage he seemed especially keyed up. This was as much as five years ago. He talked for a long time on his favorite subject, the past. Said that the past was just as real as the present, that the future was just as real as the present, and that the only thing that kept us from seeing this was the fact that our minds were tied down to the present and could only see a tiny distance forward or backward.

"I can take a trip to New York, or Berlin, or Tokyo," he said (or something like that), "so why can't I go back to New York as it was ten years ago, or to ancient Babylon, or to pay my unexpected respects to Aaron Burr or Julius Caesar? You say they're dead and gone? Gone where? Into the past? Well, then, *if one had the method,* why couldn't one go back into the past and find them? Find one's very self, for that matter,

when one was younger. You ask me what the method is? That I don't know, but I insist in the possibility!"

I made some commonplace objections and he took a new tack. Picked up a book, tossed it into the air, and caught it.

"Did you watch that, Ellis?" he asked. "Did you notice that when the book was moving fast you only got a blur? That, in other words, you were seeing it in more *places* than one and therefore more *times* than one? Do you realize what that means? You saw a little of the past of that book as it went through the air and a little of its future? Only a little? But that's enough."

Don't get impatient, Kramer, while I ramble through these seemingly impertinent matters. They have an important, but indirect bearing on the things that have been happening lately; though what kind of a bearing you'd never suspect.

Anyway, I think I agreed there was something to what he said about the book. It was late—I should have been gone long before—but he proposed a cup of coffee. There was an amused glint in his eyes as we sipped it. I remember thinking that probably my very normal and sane reactions to his unbounded speculations were a source of relief and relaxation to him.

It was about five minutes later that I began to notice there was something wrong with my eyesight. It frightened me at first. Things in motion began to blur. The cat walked into the room and out again. I rubbed my eyes but after it was gone I could still see it walking through the room, a great black trail of cat. Only slowly did it vanish. You know, how after you've looked at a bright light you can still see it after you shut your eyes? Afterimage—it was something like that. But, more than that. After I'd rubbed my eyes, I put my hands down—to find that, in spite of that, my hands were still in front of my eyes. It was some time before I could see clearly again.

Kesserich must have noticed my look of abject fear for he said to me, "Don't be alarmed, Ellis; it's just a harmless, little experiment."

I started to say, "You fool, what have you done," but before I'd got the sentence out of my mouth I realized I was still hearing what Kesserich had said a moment before and the realization struck me dumb. Kesserich, himself, was a blur. As he got up I could still see him sitting in the chair. He took up the book and threw it into the air again. I could see the path of the thing as plain as I see you.

"This time you saw a little more of the book's future and a little more of the book's past," he said with a smile, a smile that lingered on his face like the grin of a Cheshire cat.

However, by now the effect of what I realized he must have given me in the coffee was beginning to wear off. In a remarkably short time my sight and hearing were normal once again. I proceeded to become very indignant. I remembered that hashish and loco weed were supposed to have very much the same effect as I'd just experienced and I told him I strongly objected to being drugged without my knowledge and consent.

He tried to placate me.

"I'd tried to stuff on myself several times before, so I knew it was safe. I wanted to prove to you there was something in my argument and I know you think my ideas a bit too crazy for you ever to take any drug I'd brewed."

While he was still explaining how his preparation, called x-hashish, differed from what is commonly called hashish, I stormed out of the house.

After that—it was about five years ago, as I said—I began to see less and less of Kesserich. From an idler who spun romantic imaginings he was metamorphosing into an investigator with a purpose that he unswervingly pursued. He made occasional trips to libraries and universities—though I'll wager no one but myself got as much as a whisper of what he was doing. He worked for long hours each day. Every once in a while he'd bring in a new piece of apparatus. And he performed experiment after experiment, must have . . .

Quite a bit of electrical stuff, too, was delivered at his place, transformers, specially designed coils, coil forms, a tremendous quantity of wire. A heavy power line was run out to his place; there was some unusual contract that puzzled the local utility people.

A good deal of this I learned from the townspeople whom I was visiting in my professional capacity.

Kesserich became for them first an engaging mystery and then a tradition. When the electric lights would dim momentarily at night they would turn to one another and say, "Mister Kesserich's usin' the power now."

So much for old times; I jump ahead to within two months of the present. Something happened to Kesserich, the importance of which I did not, could not at the time conceive. In fact, all that came through to me were some strange stories, trivial but disturbing. For example, Kesserich had walked through town, looking at no one and singing some outlandish gibberish at the top of his voice; or, he had frightened some wandering children with a wild story and there was talk of prosecution; or, he was sitting in the graveyard laughing unrestrainedly and knelt at the tombstones—that particular incident gave Eldredge a great fright and people began to mention insanity and nod gravely. Things like that; nothing more. O yes, once I met Kesserich, but he only talked enthusiastically about college days, answered my anxious questions with laughs, and suddenly walked off like a king, reciting poetry to himself. I was worried. He didn't seem exactly insane but I sensed a deep terror and a burden, things that he seemed to be fighting with his forced, hysterical exuberance. The crisis, thought I then, that comes to certain people when they realize the inescapability of their introversion.

All it came to outwardly was a heightening of the fear and the suspicion in the townspeoples' attitude toward Kesserich.

Soon the whole episode was swept out of my mind by my life's catastrophe, my wife's death. The passing of a week found my mind still completely obsessed with thoughts of it. I could not sleep. One night, in bed and to the accompaniment of the howling of a rising wind, I set out once again on the vicious circle of fruitless speculation. If only she hadn't chosen that particular fruit . . . and so on; I think my letter must have shown you just how I was feeling.

Kramer, have you even in day-dreaming wished that your life could be shoved back a year or two so that you would be able to avoid mistakes, take advantage of vanished opportunities? That was the hopeless wish that kept circling through my mind, still hopeless, but a thousand times stronger than you've probably ever felt it. For I didn't want a past opportunity; I wanted my wife. If only I could have known, if only I could have stopped her, if only I could have

been at hand, if only . . . my helplessness almost made me burst out in an hysterical laugh.

And then . . . then I suddenly lay very still, rigid. In the mind of one in an ecstasy of joy or grief, meaningless incidents will flare up with a deep significance. It was that way with me. I thought of Kesserich sitting in a graveyard, laughing at the tombstones. That action of his seemed to sum up for me the whole of reality and—this is the strangest thing of all—filled me with an irrational hope. Perhaps I thought that Kesserich could teach me how to conquer my racking grief. We're egotists mostly, Kramer; it's our suffering that matters to us and not the thing we're suffering for. A near sleepless week had made dust of my nerve juice. God knows just why I went to Kesserich. Perhaps only to be near someone. Anyhow, I went.

I threw on my clothes, stumbled down the darkened stair, and dashed out of the house, as hurriedly as a machine gone mad. The storm had broken; great sheets of rain were driven by the high wind. I got my roadster out of the garage and rocketed through the town, out into the desert, out into chaos, out to Kesserich.

My wild knocking brought him to the door. I saw his haggard face in a lightning flash, saw its every drawn line graven momentarily and immobile as though on the statue of martyr.

"Kesserich," I said, the intensity of my feeling preventing any preliminary statement, "I've come to . . ." and I paused, speechless at my unreason.

"I think I know why," he said slowly and with a terrible irony, freezing me, the world, and himself; "Yes, yes, it had to be just this . . . just this . . ."

CHAPTER 10

THE FINAL OUTBURST

Suddenly Ellis broke off his story; with a start I became aware of small, threatening noises that my rapt attention had hitherto excluded. Noises from the outside. Then I noticed that Ellis was peering furtively at one of the windows. There was the sound of many swift footsteps, a thunderous knocking at the door. Ellis started away, reached the feet of the stairs, and paused—in doubt, it seemed from the tenor of his muttered ejaculation. I recognized the voices of the chief of police and of Elstrom in hurried conference outside the door. Then the incisive sound of an ax; the first blow shattered a panel. Quickly, I placed myself in a little alcove at one side of the door. The events of the day made me fear anything; I was not going to be found "on the spot."

As the remnants of the door were finally swung in, Ellis switched on the light. Several men, bewildered by this, checked their rush inward and stood, blinking and panting. Elstrom, who was clutching a terrified boy by the shoulder, was the first to speak.

"See, see," he screamed, the laryngitic squeak now constituting almost his entire voice, "it's just as I told you. He's here hiding, wondering what to do with his wife's body. Rather incompetent, isn't it? A *good* doctor ought to have no difficulty in disposing of a corpse."

Ellis's face was white but he held on to his composure.

"I hardly understand the meaning of this illegal intrusion," he said, ignoring Elstrom and addressing himself to the others. "I have just now returned home and cannot imagine any justification for this wild and rowdyish action. What have you to say for yourselves? You don't seem to know what you're doing."

What he said was true. It was exactly as it had been at the police station: a crowd dashing about, plunging into courses of action seemingly without any adequate motivation. But before they were forced into admitting their bewilderment, Elstrom answered for them.

"We know you poisoned your wife and were afraid that an autopsy would prove that the stuff in her stomach wouldn't tally with the stuff on my trees. You wanted people to blame me but even with that you couldn't rest easy. You were scared for your miserable life. So you stole her body. And you were aided by another miserable degenerate, your dear Mister Kesserich. I can prove it all. Robert Graves, tell what you know!"

He twisted the boy by the shoulder and held him out like

an exhibit. I started to interfere, but thought better of it, deciding to hold my hand. At the same moment I saw the Reverend Ferguson appear at the door. He, too, hesitated; however, he looked both less bewildered and more worried than the other men.

The boy's sobs were choked off by his terror and he began to speak—mechanically, as though he'd done it several times before.

"I went out in the graveyard some nights ago on a dare and I sees a light close and gets awful scared—a dim light, like goes with ghosts. Then I sees Mister Ellis here diggin' at a grave, the one you showed me. And with him was Mister Kesserich, only he . . ." here his voice broke, "looked like a ghost. All blurred-like, where his skin showed. It scared me something terrible. I run."

Because I was concealed, my senses were likely more acute and free than the others'. I heard something that I doubt disturbed any of the others' consciousnesses, even Ellis's. I heard the creak of footsteps on the floor above.

"So you sees now," came in triumphant squeak from Elstrom. "You sees now, *Doctor* Ellis. You broke my heart, stealing my little girl that I'd been as kind to as twenty husbands and then murdering her in cold blood. Got insurance on her too, didn't you? Butcher! Butcher! Have you begun to mutilate her?"

Ellis started to reply, then suddenly turned and raced up the stairs, out of sight. Elstrom followed him, puffing and screaming. The others started forward, then paused doubtfully—even the chief of police. They still moved as men in a dream, with staring eyes and gaping faces.

Elstrom reached the top, started to follow on, and then went as frozenly rigid as if he'd been plunged into liquid helium. His eyes were fixed on something, or somebody, we could not see from below. His voice rose into a terrible falsetto:

"Don't do it! Don't come! I did it for love! Don't!"

The squeak became a rattle. Then he went over backwards, to roll down the stairs, slowly, a fat sack, indented by whatever it hit. I doubt whether anyone could have thought he was still alive.

Those of the crowd that had gotten into the room stood still for full ten seconds—longer even than I had expected of their fear. The minister raised his head, looking about with strange speculativeness. I poised myself for action.

There were small, confused sounds from the floor above, then rapid footsteps on a stair; there must have been a second flight at the back of the house. The chief of police dashed toward the hall leading rearward, only to find a medium-heavy door locked. Others followed, to bring the ax into play; suddenly the leaders changed their minds and turned, evi-

dently to rush through the front door and around to the back. At the last surge forward I had moved out to stand beside the spell-bound stragglers crowding the entrance. And now I instinctively turned all my efforts to further the confusion at the door and so delay the leaders. I suppose I was partly moved by a romantic perversity in my nature that makes me always favor an outnumbered minority.

However, it was only after a few moments of pushing and panting that the leaders stumbled and plunged raggedly around the side of the house and up the drive leading to the built-in garage. Just then the flimsy doors were bumped open and a touring car shot out in screaming, roaring first. The mob scattered in time, some of them throwing themselves to the lawns on either side of the drive and landing sprawling. The gears bit into second as the machine swerved half across a lawn and onto the street. The late-comers were jumping out of the way; no one was hurt. I recognized John Ellis at the wheel. The chief of police fired a belated couple of shots but they apparently went wide.

I got away as quickly as I could. I was done up.

The next day I left Smithville; it is not my intention to return. Early in the morning I learned that Ellis's car had been pursued but with no success; he had been given too great a start by the bewildered chief of police. The house was searched that night but nothing of any suspicious character whatever was found; I imagine that it will stand empty for a few years and then be sold for taxes, unless some distant relative of Ellis's turns up or unless Ellis returns and is able to clear himself.

It turned out that we were right in thinking Elstrom dead. Two doctors would call it nothing but heart failure precipitated by unaccustomed exertion and extreme excitement; at all events and to my knowledge, no further attempts were made to apprehend Ellis in any connection. My own idea is that the town was scared back into normalcy by a fear for its own collective sanity. They wanted in the worst way to forget him. Ferguson has since substantiated this in two, long, intelligent, but comparatively noninformative letters. As far as he can learn, Smithville has ceased to be a center magnetic to the preternatural. Nevertheless, I have no desire to revisit it.

I have heard from Ellis, or at least I think I have—a scrawl from San Francisco apprising me of his safety and of a desire to let all explanations drop, especially since he claimed to be entering a new life. Something about the look of the envelope makes me think it was delayed for some time by a remailing agency. He seems to have determined on secrecy.

My memory of his college desire to become a missionary doctor makes me think he may have gone to some part of the orient. Half the time I wished he had written more and the other half I am glad that the whole Smithville problem has never been reopened.

A little of the spare money that my modest success as an author has provided me with I have used in employing a news bureau to glance through papers coming from China for news of a Dr. John Ellis. Thus far I have received only one clipping that interests me (the few others all concerned an aged British military surgeon in Shanghai). The odd one mentions a Dr. Ellis taking over a dangerous voluntary post in a plague-ridden inland province. The first name is not given and I am further inclined to doubt its being my friend because it mentions him as expecting to be joined by his wife. Doubt? God, I am not so sure . . .

For I cannot forget that as his touring-car plunged through the mob and away I saw someone crouched in the seat beside him, motionless—whether dead or alive I could not guess—but, and I am not sure of any definite reason for this opinion, seemingly a woman.

CHAPTER 11

THE BLACK CAT

Frankly, when I penned those last lines, I thought they would never be augmented, I only wanted a clear account of the single bizarre interval in my otherwise commonplace life. Then, whenever I wanted to mull the thing over, my imagination wouldn't have so great a chance of leading my memory astray. Matters, large or small, that one can't reconcile to what is reasonable, have a way of being forgotten; one begins to doubt their entire fabric. That very thing happened to me in spite of my manuscript.

The fact that John Ellis had admitted being dosed at one time (or more than once) with a mixture called x-hashish came to seem more and more important to me. That, and the nervous, feverish state he claimed to be in after his wife's death. Events prevented me from hearing all of his story but what I *did* hear of it did indeed have the quality of an opium dream; again and again I remembered that what I had read in the fragment of Kesserich's notebook made me suspect him of being a drug addict.

Worse, though, the disappearance of Mary's body and the

sudden flight of Ellis from the mob could not but give rise to suspicions it is better not to entertain of a person who has been one's friend and may still be. Today every educated person can hardly help but know of those pitiable creatures whose warped desires drive them to robbing graves. It might even be possible that Ellis killed his wife in order that—but there is no need of expanding this topic, save to note that it fits in nicely with the drug addict theory. Though I must mention that I was even inclined to give the blowing up of Kesserich's laboratory a dark interpretation. No remains identifiable as human had been found; still the explosion had been a violent one; it might have covered up traces, traces of a Kesserich who knew too much.

But how explain all the facts? The strange behavior of Elstrom and his death, which was, I feel, caused by fright; I'd swear to that impression in any court.

Then, too, what became of Ellis's other car; he had a roadster besides the touring-car in which he made his escape. This is a small point, but it has bothered me.

And why, if Ellis had murdered Kesserich, did he mistake me for him when I knocked at the door? And what was behind the boy's strange description of Kesserich as he appeared in the graveyard? And why . . . but there are no end to my "whys?" and "whats?"

As for the strange behavior of the population of Smithville,

I have since read a number of books dealing with mob psychology and the genesis of rumor. In them I have been confronted by incidents quite as bewildering to the untutored. However, even if I do accept the text-book explanation, important questions are still left unanswered. If Smithville was a case of "mob psychology," then what was the cause? What was the background? I saw people act in a completely unreasonable way; I saw a ridiculous rumor (that Mary Ellis was buried alive) spread through scores in the course of minutes; and then, from all I've heard, the unrest ended just as quickly as it began.

Now, that sort of thing doesn't "just happen." Mob psychology doesn't "just happen." There must have been something to make those people, average people, susceptible. But what could that something have been? A secret cult? But I saw no evidence of one and it's a silly, sensational idea, anyway. A master hypnotist? But that's impossible, for how could he work? And yet . . .

O, I think I'd give the thing up as a case of "mass-stupidity" if it weren't for Ferguson. He was so reasonable, so convinced and convincing . . .

Forget it.

And the trail of pebbles. Symptomatic, isn't it, that I keep overlooking that important experience? Well, when I wasn't overlooking it, I was beginning to think it some fantastic sort of optical illusion. Yes, I was willing to distrust my own senses to the point of inventing myself with a kind of minor, sporadic insanity, rather than admit a preternatural agency. That's clear isn't it?

I write this much to warn my readers against the insidious mental forces that work unceasingly to shield consciousness from a knowledge of those wild powers that walk the world unrecognized and denied by science. What I have written no longer represents my own point of view.

Yet can I be sure? Although what happened at The Black Cat seemed to be a hideously complete substantiation of my wildest hypotheses, I find myself longing to doubt its reality as much as I doubt the reality of some of the things that happened at Smithville. There is no denying the fact that I was a little drunk at the time. It is barely possible that certain repressed theories festered in my mind to such an extent that when they did appear they cloaked themselves in the form of actual event.

However, I shall write everything down just as I seem to remember it, for whenever I rise sufficiently above the petty fears and cheaply logical explanations characteristic of everyday human reasoning, I must admit that I am unable honestly to dispose of everything on the well-worn grounds of illusion and coincidence.

First, let me explain about The Black Cat. It is a quiet little drinking establishment located near the great New York university that Ellis, Kesserich, and I attended. The place has persisted into the era of repeal along with and perhaps because of its large tin mugs and generous portions. The proprietor, an aging Hungarian, is satisfied with reasonable but regular profits. He is a man of no little cultivation and like many Europeans, is an enthusiastic admirer of the writings of Edgar Allan Poe, after whose famous story he has named his establishment.

As I remember, Kesserich discovered the place and became rather acquainted with the proprietor. You see, the name Kesserich is Hungarian and even, if one goes far enough back, old Hun.

Lately, I had revisited The Black Cat quite often; not because I am a heavy drinker looking for cheap prices—an assumption that would make even my closest friends laugh—but because I find that old haunts have a way of stimulating the imagination. An author needs to keep in contact with his own past or some of his best ideas will be lost.

This winter night whose events I am going to relate found New York in the grip of an incisive cold snap. A slight snow falling, the air still, sounds clarified but reduced in number, automobiles creeping and occasionally skidding with dreamlike irrevocability on the ice-film. Partly due to the fact that the university was not in session, The Black Cat was deserted. This made me both lonely and pleased. The proprietor proposed hot rum punches. I acquiesced and he promised to brew them with meticulous care. For a while we conversed together. I realized that once again his profound understanding of the art of drinking had enabled him to find the precise liquid answer to my mood and, in my enthusiasm and gratitude, I consumed a few more glasses than were indicated as necessary, finally retiring to a secluded booth to dream. The drinking was by no means a great excess. Of that I am positive. At no time were my powers of judgment and reason seriously interfered with. However, I was sufficiently affected not to be able, for a few seconds, to determine why the face, shadowed as it was by a hat, of the man who sat down to join me uninvited, seemed vague, featureless, blurred.

Then I realized that it was covered in bandages. Completely covered from collar to hat brim. A pair of seemingly thick glasses took up the eye holes.

My surprise was not as great as may be thought. One comes in contact with so many people in New York that their variety becomes a commonplace. Besides, the appalling number of automobile accidents makes plaster casts and bandages no great novelty. "I am confronted," I reasoned logically, "either by a nut, or by some friend who seeks to surprise me or else thinks I have already heard of his misfortune."

Taking the latter hypothesis for granted I attempted to deduce the identity of the still silent stranger from traits other than facial. This proved difficult; his hands were covered with gloves, his eyes with thick, distorting glasses.

Then I heard what he was idly rapping out on the table with his knuckles. Four raps, then two . . .

The man was too tall for John Ellis. His shoulders were narrower . . . yet there was only one other who knew that signal . . .

"Kramer," he said swiftly. "Old haunts—old friends."

And then I knew that it was Daniel Kesserich.

But before I go further let me describe his voice and the strange way it affected me. This came even before I was sure that it *was* Kesserich.

Briefly, his voice had a bizarre quality, a *power,* very difficult to describe. It was as if he hummed when he spoke, as if he spoke to the accompaniment of a harsh, cacophonous, but exceedingly mighty organ, whose music I could not hear but felt I *might* hear at any moment if only I could stretch the capacity of my hearing apparatus a very little. Moreover, he seemed to be speaking softly and to be clipping his words, as if in order to conceal the very quality that so impressed me. So much for his voice. There was also something strange about his *person,* something that I was inclined to attribute to my semi-intoxicated state. He seemed, not too fat, but too thick, too *dense,* for his clothes (I know that this description cannot be anything but enigmatical; however, it is the best I can do).

Rousing myself from the abstraction into which I had fallen, I greeted Kesserich with a calmness that was almost casual; a manifestation of that unconscious care and paradoxical fact characteristic of certain stages of slight intoxication.

Apparently my calmness put his mind at ease, for he leaned back in his chair and ceased to drum nervously on the table.

All agog now and determined not to scare him off with questions (he was ever the sensitive recluse), I asked him if he would join me in a drink. He immediately refused and, further, made me promise not to call the proprietor and, if he happened to approach our booth on his own initiative, to warn him off in some way. I agreed. There was in any case little chance of being overheard or even observed, the proprietor being distinguished by an almost morbid tact.

These things having been settled, Kesserich burst forth in a torrent of questions, some of which surprised me greatly for they dealt with things that any person might have read in the newspaper. However, it did set me thinking that he might have been suffering from a temporary loss of memory, an aphasia dating possibly from some shock that might have occurred in Smithville.

But when I started to answer his questions it was only a moment before he jerked his hands at me in a peculiarly irritated gesture, grimaced quickly, and said, "It's futile. Don't try."

Put at a loss by this attitude I let slip the question that had been teetering on my lips: "What was it, Kesserich, that happened to you at Smithville?"

He stiffened, looked at me, then sank back, saying, "No, no; there are things . . . a person could not think reasonable . . . unless he saw; besides . . ."

Again I marveled at the strangeness of Kesserich's voice. It seemed to have acquired a timbre and a humming quality that were, to me, unique. Perhaps it was due to my own condition; I noticed I was still having a little trouble with my eyes.

"There's something you don't know," I pressed on. "It's this: I saw with my own eyes things that were in no way reasonable." And I told him of my experience with the pebbles and of the beginning of Ellis's story.

There upon he laughed with a kind of sardonic woe and, "that it should happen to you. O, that it should happen to you. That puts all three of us in the same boat. All three: you,

Ellis, and myself. Should I tell you the rest? Why not? You could even make a story of it," here his laughter took on an almost unearthly convulsiveness, "and then no one would ever, ever believe it! Men would say that it would be impossible and, were *the method* ever rediscovered, minds would be forewarned and able to forget it; forget it at all costs. Yes, yes, yes, it is the way of all ways to keep the secret!"

And when his chuckles died, he began.

Only at one point was his conversation interrupted, or, rather, almost interrupted. That was when I heard the gentle tread of the proprietor's step approaching our table. However, at the time, I had not been so gripped by what I was listening to, I might have speculated upon why the footsteps moved off at a shuffle that was almost a run. Perhaps the old Hungarian saw something that I, in my drunkenness . . . no matter; my task now is to reproduce Kesserich's conversation.

CHAPTER 12

KESSERICH: AN AFTERMATH

(THE STATEMENT OF THE MAN WITH THE BANDAGED FACE)

So Ellis broke off his story at the crucial moment? Crucial for you. Characteristic of him; always had a way of messing things. Messed me—by making Mary his wife. I could try to unmess it. Probably succeed. No matter.

Know what I'm doing now, Kramer? Remember your old argument? One I used to dispute. That science was progressing fast, geometrical rate, and would inevitably discover a way of destroying the world. Well, you're right. Must admit it. Especially since I'm devoting my whole life to squelching science's advance in certain directions.

All because I chanced on that damned electrical trick.

Chanced, I say. Couldn't be gotten at by a theoretical approach. Firmly convinced that the theory, if one's possible, is a thousand years ahead of us. Maybe not so far though; anyway, I didn't understand it. Just chanced on it. One in a million.

Did Ellis tell you about the apparatus? You must have seen the power line yourself. Way I got started is this:

Well-known fact that when an electric field is jolted,

shifted suddenly, there's an infinitesimal energy loss. Where does this energy go? No one knows. I think to find out. By pure chance discover a terribly complex arrangement of fields that makes the loss surprisingly great. Great enough to make objects in the field disappear when the jolt comes. Where do they go? Difficult to say, but I find a way of making them come back by subtly reversing shift. Come back from where? The scientist shrugs his shoulders and experiments further. The young wizard is excited. Things like x-hashish seem less than toys.

My reasons for all this hectic activity? My old desire to get the better of time. Why not walk it like space? Acrobatically minded youngster, was Kesserich. Little knowing the things that walk the inner ways of the world. Asking for it.

My general theory? In broad, sweeping gestures. Thusly, gentlemen, does the Herr Professor believe: that we people can move in our three-dimensional world because we have some thickness, be it slight, in time, in the fourth dimension. That is, we comprise in ourselves a little future and a little past, we are four-dimensional worms; that's old stuff.

Next step: How are we to move in time, the fourth dimension?

Answer by analogy obvious, namely: to achieve some thickness, be it however slight, in *supertime;* that is, in the *fifth dimension;* the dimension that is to our time as our time

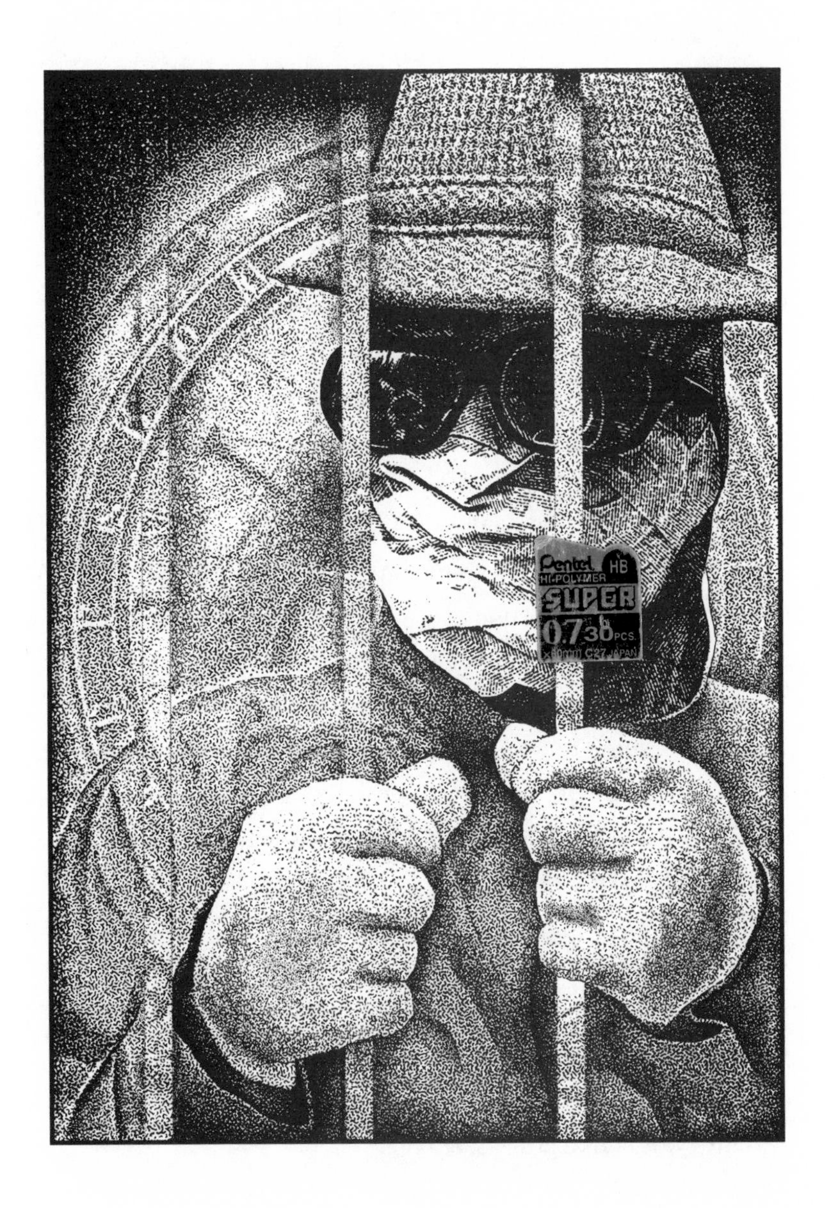
Pentel
HB
HI-POLYMER
SUPER
0.7
30 PCS.

is to our space. Don't bother if you can't picture it to yourself; I was once as badly off.

But what's all this loose talk got to do with the energy loss resulting from the field jolt? That's the question you ought to ask me. Here's the way my thought went:

The field jolt invests local time with inertia; the time in the field slows up. That is, whatever's in the jolted field has its time thicknesses pile up on one another; a drag, an accumulation like that of snow on a snowball rolling in snow. What then? When the pile gets big, its pressure gets big and something has to give. Something does give, namely resistence in the direction of supertime, the fifth dimension. Objects in that jolted field have a new body created for them, a five-dimensional body. They begin to move in supertime and are therefore free to move in the old fourth-dimension time just as if it were space. They can go back into the dead past or forward into the dead future. I say dead because our past and our future are changeless with respect to supertime; it's only when you move in ordinary time that you think there's a difference between the past and the future; actually both are equally predetermined and predestined. We live in a universe that is, as you might say, frozen in four dimensions; our universe is located in a calm of dimensional activity; it is like cross-section of . . .

But why should I drivel on, trying to make you understand what I don't? Anyhow, you've read part of my diary. In short, I found in my jolting electric fields, a method of giving people access to the future and the past. People, I say. Tried animals first to see if it was reasonably safe. And access, I say, not transportation. Once through, one had to walk. Walk back across ordinary time. Imbecile. Magnificent. That diary you got hold of describes my first experiences. I was in a hurry and only made sure that the pages describing my apparatus would be burned. Anyhow, you've read it; can imagine my wonder. So I'll skip ahead. Never have time for details. Even now.

Mary Ellis's death. I loved her, Kramer. Wanted her. And when she died I saw a way. I could go back in time. Had already done that twice. I would go back to the orchard where she died *as it was just before her death!* I would remove the cause of her death, the poison on the fruit. That would make her future course through space-time living and not dead. Do you begin now, Kramer, to see the powers of a fifth-dimensional creature? He can change the past or the future just as easily as you or I change the present. Mary Ellis couldn't be dead with source of death—poison—removed. Removed by me, Kesserich.

That would win her, make her love me. Kesserich a god,

resurrecting the woman he loved. She his god-bride. Both on a level above the common herd. Common herd, including one John Ellis, her husband.

Rotten delusion, all of it. I'm no god, only member of the common herd, member who stumbled on a grandiose discovery. And so that other member of the common herd, one John Ellis, husband, comes to claim his own.

Why did he come on the night of nights, night I was going back, like a hero or saint, to Mary? Ironic coincidence? Telepathy? Jealous warp in space-time? Which? Can't guess.

Come he did. Just as he told you. In a storm. To my door, knocking.

Why didn't I send him about his business? Easiest thing in the world, you'd think, but I couldn't. I was beginning to break, go to pieces, all that. The godlike power was too great for lucky member of common herd, one Daniel Kesserich. The sight of Ellis, distracted, made me feel like just another child. Had to tell him everything; had to! Would have gone to pieces from sheer weight of responsibility otherwise. I couldn't stand the coincidence of his coming just when he did.

We both went through, through the path that leads to future and past. Had to take Ellis along, share everything with him, all responsibilities. No initiative left, but still the desire to rescue the woman I loved, even if it was for another.

About my machine for getting through? That's one thing I don't talk about. It's both simple and complicated; though it wasn't much to look at, outside of the coils. You just stood in a field of force that was jolted automatically by a time-operated control. There was something about the automatic control in my diary, wasn't there? That was what made it possible for one to get back, to slough his five-dimensional body. After one got through, time control automatically reversed the direction of the field jolt. What happened then was just the opposite of what happened when one went through. Ordinary time pressure, instead of being increased, was diminished. To relieve this look of pressure, this time-vacuum, there came a flow from the fifth dimension . . . so all one had to do was to relocate the field of force . . . and wait for the jolt. . . . You see?

Sensations on going through? Described in what you read in my diary. Everything opened up immensely, like coming out of a narrow tunnel. As if the world had been as thin as paper before; only now it took on thickness. Could see my room, my laboratory, stretching out into past and future, alternating day and night. Also, time when there was no house there, only desert; could only see that dimly; a blurring effect.

I'm reminded of another thing: the terrible inertia. Hard for us to walk, hard to make any movement; must be similar to feelings a diver has when undersea. Remember that. Inertia! Got it? Important. Very important point.

How really to describe it? I can't. Impossible. Lack proper words, adjectives. Could walk in regular space, or into future or past, or both ways at once. Why weren't we noticed in Smithville? Because I was careful that we always kept to the past and never touched on the present. A change in our own bodies? There must have been one, but we couldn't notice it since our sense organs changed at the same time our bodies did. Partakers of the super-dimension, the fifth. Something no person or thing in our world has. Divine power—as you will see. God. Idiots.

Ellis takes it calmly enough. The calm of shock. Emotions exhausted. Having something to do that takes up all the energy left, nothing startles him.

Then comes the trip to the orchard where Mary ate the poisoned fruit. Our objective. We walk, we plunge, we plow through the past, and through space. Both ways at once. I said that before. Sometimes it's night; sometimes day. Remember, we have to go back more than a week in time. But I can't describe what it felt like. All blurs and is hard to remember, like the things that beat on the sense organs of a newborn baby.

We leave our track by pebbles that I'd pocketed before. Might get lost. O yes, those were the pebbles that you saw appear and that so surprised you. As soon as we'd dropped them they began to grow into the future. At a definite rate. Also the footprints. You mentioned seeing one appear, didn't you? You see, you just got there when it chanced to catch up with the present. Different time rate. Don't know the exact difference, except it's different from ordinary time rate. No matter.

Important thing is that pebbles and footprints *did* catch up with the present. Everything we five-dimensional hybrids did in the past had its effect on the present. Ellis tossed a pebble away once. Know what happened—'spite of the inertia? It sped into the future and hit a woman named Peterson. Ellis had to iodine her later. You read about it?

Damned nerve-racking, as you can see. Anything we did might have its effect, good or bad, on the present. Godlike powers. I step on a worm back in the past and wreck an empire, maybe. Can't tell what the results of the simplest actions will be. Powers like that too much for member of common herd, one Kesserich.

Anyhow, we find the fruit that poisoned Mary. Locate it by spotting Mary. Her body stretching out of the past into the future, all continuous. Four-dimensional worm. Even at that Ellis wants to grab her. I hold him; keep telling him that we mustn't touch more than we absolutely need to touch. It is becoming an obsession with me already. Afraid of those delightfully godlike powers. Naughty Kesserich, don't touch!

I will only let Ellis wipe and cleanse the fruit she ate with his handkerchief. You saw that handkerchief too, didn't you? All popped out of the past for your wondering gaze.

Have him cleanse the fruit—that is, the fruit as it was before she ate it, but after it had been sprayed. Strangely difficult job for even a five-dimensional Ellis.

Why all these precautions? Your eyes ask me, Kramer, why? Why didn't we take her back to the present from a time at which she was still living? Impossible, I tell you. Would mean taking a three-dimensional section out of her four-dimensional body. For now it was four-dimensional to us, a four-dimensional time-snake. Take a whole Mary out of that? A whole Mary, neither more nor less? Impossible. Like trying to cut a single cell out of a human organ with the aid of a butcher knife. We had no four-dimensional surgical instruments. We had to be clever instead.

So we cleansed the fruit and then went ahead in time to where Mary lay dead. Watching, watching for a result. Praying. Wonder lost in anxiety.

Then it came. A flush on her death-pale face. A flush, delicate, but a flush. It went through me like light. A miracle! Daniel Kesserich had performed a miracle!

Then anxiety and worry close in around my godlike feeling. I have performed a miracle, yes, but I have not rescued

Mary. What is it to the member of the common herd, Kesserich, that he has, by luck and luck alone, stumbled on a miracle? The woman he loves is not yet safe; safe for another, yes, but safe.

What to do? What to do? It is the time for caution, stupendous caution. Every move we make changes the future by changing the past. A false step and we wreck—wreck anything, we know not what, perhaps our own lives. For yes! A man can go back and change his own past and so himself. We are as children in an evil land of faery, Ellis and myself. A false step and Mary, living again, goes forward to die again in a smothering grave or under an embalmer's knife. I remember she was not embalmed—that is one thing I worry about.

But the grave. We have made her alive, but will that life reach the present? And if it reaches the present it will find her in the grave. Will we be able to rescue her before that new life is blotted out? Or will the future be changed more radically? Will we go back to find that she had never died, that there has been no death, no funeral, that she still lives as ever. I think not. There is an inertia that works against those changes one makes in the past, especially if they be changes in the thoughts of living creatures. As if nature abhors those lawless changes of the past as she abhors the time-vacuum. She makes them die out, if she can.

If she can!

She will kill the reborn Mary, if she can!

There is but one thing to do. One lone course having a chance in its favor, though all other chances be against it. We cannot take the living Mary out of her four-dimensional body. We cannot tamper further. We must go back to the present and get the body of Mary out of the grave, then wait for the life we gave her to catch up with that lifeless body we steal.

Begging with Ellis, commanding, finally dragging, I bring him back along the trail of pebbles, through space and time, to my laboratory.

We stand in the field of force.

How do we, on the five-dimensional side, locate the right *time,* as well as place, in which we stand and await the automatic returning jolt? Simple. We find the trail of our own bodies in space, the bodies we have left. We find a time-break in those bodies, a missing segment in the four-dimensional worm. What is that missing segment? It is the spot from which we departed. So—it is also the spot at which there is room for us to return, at which the force-field is operating.

But the waiting for the return. Nerve-racking. The device is untested, too new; there is always a hideous danger. Then the rush of force; for the first time I feel its crude power and am afraid—but then we are back in the present; the break naturally keeps up with the present, you see.

Sobbing with relief, yet dazed, we stare at one another across the blessedly commonplace laboratory. There is something strange in the look Ellis gives me; it is only later that I find out what it means.

It was night when we went through. Now day is breaking. All day we must wait; only at night can we steal the body. For it must be stolen; there is no other way. Why? All day long Ellis pleads and insists that we get, somehow, an order for exhumation. I dissuade him. I know what will happen. He is excited in no ordinary way. He will blab out his hopes. What will the common herd authorities make of those hopes? Insanity, at least. There will be delays; Ellis will grow more wildly insistent with them. They will call doctors; he will fight. Then the lock-up, the asylum. For me, too, if I insist on the exhumation with him, if I support his story.

No! We must wait. I have a pickax and spade. By night we may enter that graveyard, enter it even before the gates close, and steal the body. The place is then deserted; it is simple.

How I guessed that our fifth-dimensional activities had not canceled Mary's death and funeral altogether? I looked at the back issues of the local papers; they still contained articles, announcements. Besides, I was intuitively sure.

With arguments and with force I restrain Ellis. At twilight, for the dark comes suddenly, we go by lonely ways, carrying spade and pickax muffled in cloth. The car we do not take; it is still too early for that. Remember, we are to become heinous criminals in the eyes of Smithville—if they see us. I would have waited longer, but that he will not do, so I must acquiesce or lose all chances.

We manage to be left in the graveyard when the sexton goes. I am almost seen but escape detection. Then our task; five feet of sandy dirt. Ellis works madly; it is soon completed. We jimmy the lead lid and then—Ellis greens. For it is death he sees. Death and decay. Damned are his hopes. But not mine. I had expected as much. Her new life is not yet caught up with the present.

So we get the body to his house. He has to fetch the car he left at my laboratory. While he is gone I replace coffin, earth, sod, and footstone. That last I must have put in backwards, as your sharp eyes discovered. Mistake. Then to his house we take the fearful body of the woman we both love. We place her in her bed. Shuddering, we descend the stair. We must wait. I do not know for how long. I am weak with reaction. The problems involved in the proper use of my great discovery come back upon me, a leaden burden.

I pour us whiskey. After Ellis gulps his glass he looks at me. For the first time the awful tension has left his face, the

tension that had seemed almost to merge into the strain of madness, so he looks at me. Then there comes into his eyes a horror, a horror that I have seen trace of before.

"Kesserich," he cries, "what has happened to you? Have you given me that drug again?"

I laugh. But he still stares. Then I look at myself, my hands and arms. They are no different. I regard Ellis suspiciously. He must be mad indeed, I think. Then there comes a doubt. Could he see something that I do not see?

I remember that when we were jerked back into the normal world, the world of the present, I felt a spasm that I'd never noticed going through alone. I also remember that that time, the time the two of us came back, I gave him the more favorable position in the field of force. I may be . . . my head swims, the world trembles, ghostly and insubstantial, before my eyes; the stupidly staring Ellis is becoming a man of gas, whom the next breath may dissipate. . . . Suddenly I cannot bear to be with him, to be in the house, to think, speculate, plot, or worry further.

Without giving him a word of explanation I go out the door, take his roadster, and drive off through the blackness following the false dawn.

He has another car, if he needs it. And as for Mary, I can do no further; he is the doctor.

I am miles away when I begin to think again. On the edge

of the next town west. Thinking! I was doomed always to think again. Again I wonder . . . could it have been anything but the projection of his overwrought condition that Ellis saw? It may indeed be that I am subtly changed, that I have an improper time thickness, that I brought some of the clogging fifth dimension back with me, and that I cannot notice it because my sense organs have changed as I have changed. And that what I see shivers before my eyes, as if the world were thin, translucent. The few sounds of morning are weak and far away. Only I am real, corporeal. . . .

The sun is almost up. I am in a residential section of the town. Along the sidewalk comes a man, one whose work makes him rise early. An idea comes to me, an idea for a test. I draw up the car. I wait 'til he gets alongside, then step out and make some polite and commonplace inquiry. He starts to answer, looks at me. Then his face pales and his eyes grow wide; with a low squeal of horror he turns and runs.

I know. What Ellis saw is indeed true. I am deformed; my face, my body, even my voice is blurred, is too thick. Even as the world now seems too thin to me, I seem too solid to the world. A man of stone in a world of men of air. Almost a ghost—not because I am insubstantial but because I am *too substantial.* No longer will the common herd recognize me. I bear upon my person the stigmata of my own discovery. Always will I be the inhuman one.

The man who ran from me is far away and has turned for a second look. Slowly I re-enter the car and drive off down a lonely desert road, one that I have traveled before when I wanted a new loneliness to stir my thoughts. Only this time it is for last thoughts, for retrospect.

Ellis I have forgotten, and Mary too. Why should I remember her, or go back to her, even if the improbable should happen and she should live? Her new life would be for him and not for me. What would it mean to me to learn that my discovery had worked another miracle? It would only be another. I am sated with miracles.

And what was Mary herself to me more than a dream? She were best remain a dream.

I drive aimlessly, stopping often, letting no one see me. At night I get gas, sleep for a while in the car. But the stars are no longer my comforters; they, too, are thin.

A day passes, maybe two. I do not return. Think. Think.

It is not my deformity, my stigmata, that weighs me down; that I can dispose of with another time-trip. Other things have a greater pressure, a pressure that has rolled up with the years.

I know, Kramer, know with the certainty of an army of hitherto half-hidden thoughts, that my discovery is too big a thing for me, too big a thing for all mankind, perhaps too big for God.

Am I the man to determine what in the past should be changed? Is any man wise enough to say, "This shall be resurrected; this shall be blotted out?" And more, when I do tamper with the past, I have no way of knowing what the results of that tampering will be. I may go back to blot out a tyrant, a dictator, and find that by so doing I only make room for a worse to step in his place. I may go back to resurrect a great man who died too young and only find that it was a blessing that his death came when it did. I have the power; yes, I have the power; it weighs upon me like the world on Atlas. But have I the wisdom to use that power? No! There Daniel Kesserich remains the member of the common herd into which an irrevocable fate bore him. Were I to try to improve the world with my discovery I know, know with only too dismal a clarity, that I will only wreck what I am trying to help. And if I give or lose the power to another? That will let hell loose. For even Kesserich, miserable malign fool that he is, is an angel in comparison with most of the brutes of his herd.

O, I am weary to death with the responsibility of it. I am too small, or too tired, to thrill with the grandeur of a new vision of power. Perhaps I have been recluse and introvert because I have been afraid of what the compulsive mischievous evils in myself would do to others. Fear of living, of reality. So the modern mind-doctors might say. No matter.

Along the desert road I drive Ellis's car. Going nowhere; circling back.

Then, as it had to be, there began to throb through my brain words, implacable, unending, like a drum-beat, louder and louder:

"Destroy and escape; destroy and escape; destroy your discovery; destroy your machine; before it is too late; while you still have the power; destroy; destroy; destroy . . ."

It is possible; I have provided for this contingency days before, when something hidden in me saw it coming; I have a chemical bomb. . . .

"Destroy; destroy; destroy . . ."

Suddenly, I jerk the car around and tear off for Smithville. Driving wildly, thoughtlessly, that I may get to my laboratory while my resolution holds.

I have all planned. I will make one last trip through, to rid myself of my deformity. Then . . . destroy.

I arrive in the afternoon. I manage it. Plant the bomb. Must have been while you were following the new-appearing pebble trail to the orchard. I make a rough fuse . . .

And I succeeded. I blew up my discovery. But I did not make the last trip through; I did not rid myself of my deformity. I had lost nerve; perhaps I was afraid of what I might do to the world from the other side, afraid of what a madman might do from the other side. More, though, I could not bear, at the last moment, to do away with my last tangible tie to my greatness, the mark my discovery had put upon my very body. Saints hate to part with their stigmata; my time-thickness somehow seemed to set me, not only apart from, but also above my herd.

Now it is about all I have left. You see, I could not reduplicate my discovery. So much depended on chance, and my memory for the finer points is pretty well gone.

After seeing the explosion succeed I drove off again into the desert. I knew Ellis had another car and would not mind the loss of his roadster.

I did not want to know whether Mary had been reborn. It would be better for me to think I might have failed; that might help me to believe that my discovery had been a practical failure. I knew that if I saw her return to life I would be tempted into becoming once again a god-fool of fools.

I bought gas and supplies at night. Wore gloves; on my face bandages and glasses. Finally established myself in a lonely spot in the mountains. I managed.

Had to keep under cover. Should I be discovered, I might prove a nine-days' horror; newspapers call me "the blurred terror." Then capture. Imagine the outcry. False charges by frightened hysterics. Scientists coming from far and near to see the wonderful freak, to experiment upon him. Take samples of blood, skin, hair; they would try to put the fourth and fifth dimensions in a test tube or under a microscope. And some clever one would succeed; "Blood Test Yields Secret of the Blurred Man, Freak Proves Theory of Four-Dimensional Universe."

And then the world would be through. Having such clues, men would find the way back to the past, and then wreck the world because of their clumsiness, because of their mental limitations.

Perhaps they will do it anyway. Perhaps it is futile that I hide myself. Any day I expect to see a headline (actually I seldom get a newspaper) saying: "Noted Scientist Goes Back in Time; The Resurrection Is at Hand, Says Prelate." And then I will merely be the fool who found, and renounced, world power.

But my hope is that science will fail, that no one will ever again have my luck if I keep secret all the clues. In a few decades barbarism will be coming again and the search for the truth about matter will be waning.

Lately, though, I have become careless. Have come to New York. Live most of the time as a bandaged invalid. Draw money by mail. Take pleasure, now, in playing with the idea of having my deformity discovered. Self-doubt again, even of my deepest convictions. What matter? My way of committing suicide.

That, Kramer, is the story. Strange, I think I can see in

your eyes that you believe it. Finishing touches? About Elstrom? Where he came in? Can't you explain that? Why, the senile sadist poisoned Mary because he loved her even after she'd been married. And the idea grew upon him like a canker. Just like him to figure out a cunning way of making it all look like an accident and of shifting the blame for that accident onto a hired hand. Elstrom probably met her secretly in the orchard, gave her a specially poisoned fruit. No one to know.

What happened to the town to account for those wild, senseless actions on the part of almost everyone? That "mass-insanity," as you called it? Why, they were affected by what we did in the past; just as Mary was. False memories began to creep into their minds, memories of Mary alive, yet in her coffin. Very like, as you and Ferguson noticed, the phenomenon of post-hypnotic suggestion. A little more change and they'd have forgotten her death altogether. But they didn't. That's where the dimensional inertia I mentioned came in. It was only enough to produce false memories, fill them all with a wild guilt, a belief that they'd all had a hand in a plot to bury a woman alive. Nothing more.

The night of the riotous attack on Ellis? Elstrom was scared stiff. He, too, was beginning to feel that Mary wasn't dead. But with him it took the form of a fear that she would rise from the grave and denounce him. So he tried to use the testimony of a graveyard-wandering boy to put the blame on Ellis and me.

His death? Kramer, you said yourself that you heard footsteps on the floor above, footsteps that couldn't have been mine or Ellis's. In that case, when Elstrom went upstairs he saw something that no one ever really saw before. He saw a ghost. The resurrected Mary. The terror he feared but knew could not come, came and killed him.

Yes, I must have succeeded in saving her, so that she might look at her murderer with justice in her grave-yellow face. But today Mary is far away from me and the dream of her from my soul.

She and Ellis. I suppose they went to China, as you think. Perhaps she with still a taint of corruption. At least they came off with unwrecked lives. Human or vampire, alive or living dead, to them a miracle rightly happened. But me, Kesserich? What is a miracle to me? And what are the doings of the other living dead?

Shall I take off for you, Kramer, the bandages about my face, the gloves from my hands, the thick glasses from over my eyes? Shall the tragedian come before the audience without his mask? And prove . . . no, for you there shall be left the loophole for doubt. . . .

Good-bye, Kramer.

POSTSCRIPT

How long it was that I sat in the booth in the grip of a trembling reaction after the man with the bandages had gone I do not know. Only I too finally departed without a sight of the proprietor.

For three days I mulled my doubts and fears. What I had seen and heard must have been delirium, drunken delirium, nothing else and yet it fitted. Fitted all the facts. Impossible, but consistent.

The third day I went back to The Black Cat to settle for the drinks. As soon as the old Hungarian saw me his jaw sagged a little, his face seemed to turn pale. Yet I did not sense that it was I whom he feared, but rather something my presence suggested. He spoke no word as I paid him, only clucked his tongue, as though he wanted to mention something but was uncertain how to begin. I remembered the shuffling, fleeing footsteps I had heard on that night . . .

"I know," I said, turning in the door, "three nights ago you saw something more than a man called Kesserich."